A HAPPY ENDINGS WEDDING

KYLIE GILMORE

Copyright © 2019 by Kylie Gilmore

All rights reserved. No part of this publication may be reproduced, distributed, or transmitted in any form or by any means, including photocopying, recording, or other electronic or mechanical methods, without the prior written permission of the writer, except in the case of brief quotations embodied in critical reviews and certain other noncommercial uses permitted by copyright law.

This is a work of fiction. Names, characters, places, brands, media, and incidents are the product of the author's imagination or are used fictitiously. The author acknowledges the trademarked status and trademark owners of various products referenced in this work of fiction, which have been used without permission. The publication/use of these trademarks are not authorized, associated with, or sponsored by the trademark owners. Any resemblance to actual events, locales, or persons, living or dead, is purely coincidental.

A Happy Endings Wedding: © 2019 by Kylie Gilmore

Cover design by Sweet 'N Spicy Designs

Published by: Extra Fancy Books

ISBN-13: 978-1-942238-70-6

For you, Goddess! Enjoy catching up with the club!

1

Destination wedding to die for? Check.

Top bridal magazines *Luxury Weddings* and *Bride Special* covering the event of the century? Check. Eep!

Tying the knot with the gorgeous romantic love of her life? Triple check.

Hailey Adams dabbed at the joyful tears leaking from her eyes, careful not to ruin her eye makeup. Geez, she'd been so emotional lately. Thank goodness it was nearly the end of her workday on a Friday. It wouldn't do to meet a client while looking a mess.

She supposed her emotional state was to be expected now that *she* was finally the bride. She was a wedding planner and wanted her wedding to be the shining example, the wedding to top all weddings. She'd put heart and soul and so-o-o much time—a whole year—into planning it, and now it was almost here. In three weeks she'd be married on Villroy Island, a royal kingdom off the coast of France. Their wedding would be the inaugural wedding to launch Villroy as a premiere destination-wedding locale, saving the struggling island's economy and preserving their long proud history. No pressure.

She let out a shuddering breath and then laughed a little as her dog Rose, a white terrier-Chihuahua mix, went up on her hind legs from Hailey's lap, rested her paws on Hailey's shoulders and licked her tears. Max, a black shih tzu-Chihuahua mix, dropped his chew toy and ran over, standing on Hailey's leg, wanting in on the action. She scooped him up and cuddled them both close. Rose and Max loved each other and her. And they were crazy for Josh, who always had some special treat or toy for them.

She arranged them both on her lap and sighed. Her business partner, Ally, was out shopping for some items for an unusual Halloween wedding, so it was just Hailey in their shared office. She and Ally were now equal partners in Clover Park's premier wedding planning service, Love Junkies. They attracted die-hard romantics looking for a traditional wedding (Hailey's specialty) and unconventional brides looking for something a little different (Ally's specialty). Ally also pitched a special add-on, a sologamy ceremony (women committing to themselves) as a female bonding and empowerment event. It was a tremendously satisfying joint venture. And now Hailey had more free time to enjoy being engaged to the most wonderful man in the world.

The phone rang. She shifted to get both dogs off her lap, and then she smiled as she picked up the phone, because people could hear a smile in your voice. "Love Junkies, Hailey Adams speaking."

"Hi, Hailey. It's Camille from JH Bridal." Camille was one of the top wedding gown designers in New York City. The one-of-a-kind gown had been a gift from Hailey's friend, movie star Claire Jordan.

"Yes, hi, Camille! How're you?" She had an appointment to pick up her gown tomorrow. Maybe they had some last-minute fabulous detail they wanted to add. The gown was already incredible from the satin and lace bodice to the hand-sewn seed pearls to the beautiful long train. Camille had gone beyond Hailey's wildest fantasies, which said a lot because Hailey was intimately familiar with gorgeous wedding gowns in her line of work.

"Not so good. Hailey, I'm so sorry to bring you this news, but there was a fire, and I'm afraid your dress is ruined."

She froze, gripping the phone tighter. "A fire," she echoed. "Is everyone okay?"

"Yes, thank you. We put it out quickly, but I'm afraid the smoke has damaged your gown beyond repair."

She stared blankly in complete shock. No gown! But she was leaving in only two weeks! She and Josh had planned to arrive a week before their wedding to visit Paris. She stood and paced the office. This could *not* be happening. No gown for the inaugural wedding to be featured in *Luxury Weddings* and *Bride Special*? She couldn't just pick up something off the rack! It had to be spectacular. It had to be perfect. She'd been planning for a year so that every single thing was perfect. She'd never considered a fire. Why hadn't she considered it? She should've planned for every eventuality.

Major fail. She halted abruptly, pressing a hand to her forehead and closing her eyes.

"Hailey, did you hear what I said? You're welcome to come in tomorrow and look at the remaining inventory. It won't be an original design, but I'm sure we can find something you'll like. We'll get it fitted for you on an expedited basis."

"Thank you, Camille. I appreciate that. Good night."

She hung up and burst into tears. The dogs rushed her legs, their little paws lifting to be picked up. She looked down at them, the black fur of Max and the white fur of Rose swimming in front of her eyes. She needed Josh. He was her rock—steady and stable and strong. It was what she loved most about him. She craved that kind of stability after her unstable childhood with her single flaky mom unexpectedly left them homeless. Twice.

She clipped the leashes on the dogs and locked up for the night, walking briskly out the door, across the street, and down the sidewalk to the Happy Endings bar. Josh owned the bar and had named it for her, based on her Happy Endings Book Club and her own obsession with finding everyone a happy ending. And now what kind of happy ending was this wedding going to be without the dress of her dreams?

She scooped up both dogs in her arms before entering the

busy bar and restaurant. Her fur babies were both certified as therapy dogs, which meant they could go just about anywhere, but she was mindful not to let them run loose. The dining area to her right was filled with families enjoying dinner, the bar straight ahead filled with chatting people blowing off steam after the long work week. Friday night was the busiest time for the bar, along with Saturday night, especially now that Josh had built an addition on the back with a dance floor, an old-fashioned jukebox, and two pool tables. She'd spent many a happy time here with him and her friends. Hot tears stung her eyes again.

Stop that. You are a warrior. You will move forward with a solution, and this will still be the wedding of the century.

Josh always called her his warrior princess, which meant a lot because he was an actual warrior. He'd spent years as a paratrooper in the army, engaged in hand-to-hand combat. He loved her fighting spirit, and she fully claimed her badassery now.

She pushed through the crowd at the bar and called to Josh, who was working as bartender. He turned, a slow smile lighting up his gorgeous face, his brown eyes crinkling at the corners. His dark brown hair was close-cropped on the sides, longer on top and sexily rumpled. He was wearing the new black T-shirt she'd bought him. He lived in T-shirts and jeans, but some of them were so old they were falling apart.

"Do you have a minute?" she asked, her voice cracking under the strain of being a warrior princess with a serious wedding gown problem.

He stopped smiling, nodded once, and pulled out his phone. He was calling for backup. A moment later, Brian came out of the kitchen and took over for Josh.

She met Josh at the end of the bar, where he set a warm hand on the small of her back and led her through the kitchen to his back office. As soon as he shut the door behind them, she put the dogs down, and they immediately rushed to a box of dog toys Josh left in the corner for them.

He smoothed a lock of her hair behind her ear. "What's wrong, sweetheart?"

Her throat closed at the sweet term of endearment. Her gruff and tough former soldier used sweet words very sparingly, though she never doubted his love. "I just wanted to let you know…" Her voice broke. She took in a shuddering breath. "There's been a small hiccup." Tears leaked out, and she dashed at them with her fist. "Sorry, I've been so emotional lately with the wedding coming up so soon."

He pulled her into his arms. "Yeah, I've noticed. I'm not sure it's the wedding."

Her head shot up to look at him. "Of course it's the wedding. It's my first time as a bride. There's a lot of pressure with the magazine coverage and launching Villroy's new venue."

He slid a hand under her long hair, cupping the back of her neck and drawing her close for his kiss. "Hailey, love."

She choked on a small sob at *love*, another unusually sweet term of endearment. He must be using all these sweet words because she looked like she was about to lose it. She *was* about to lose it. "What?" she asked in a strained voice. "You're wonderful."

He smiled against her lips. "You're wonderful too. Remember when we celebrated the one-year anniversary of our engagement four weeks ago?" What a silly question. Of course she remembered. She'd planned the whole thing. They'd retraced their courtship from a pretend fight at Happy Endings bar to a clandestine passionate meeting in this very office, finishing with a romantic dinner at home. He'd done his part cooking a gourmet dinner, giving her roses, and texting her earlier in the week, letting her know how much he was looking forward to everything. He'd even made liberal use of exclamation points in his texts to show his enthusiasm, which he knew she loved.

She smiled through watery eyes. "Yes, it was awesome."

He picked her up by the waist and set her on his desk. She didn't even let out a squeak. Josh often manhandled her body and she quite enjoyed it. He pushed her dress up by her hips, spread her legs, and stood between them. She went damp in anticipation as his fingers gripped her hair, tilting her head up, his eyes heated and locked on hers. Her lips parted, all of her focus on him, her earlier distress temporarily forgotten.

A breathless moment of charged silence passed before his mouth sealed over hers in a deep, hungry kiss as he slowly lowered her to the desk. She wrapped her arms around his neck, losing herself in the delicious heat. The kiss turned carnal as he ground against her, and she moaned against his mouth. They were animals, igniting at every touch, passion and deep love binding them together. She loved it. She always wanted what he could give.

She wrapped her legs around him, lifting her hips for more. His lips shifted to her ear, his teeth giving her earlobe a tug before he whispered, "You remember this part of our anniversary? How we got carried away? So hot you couldn't wait. You begged me, Hailey. And what did I say?"

Her eyes flew open. It had been exactly like this during their engagement anniversary courtship reenactment—her on the desk; Josh on top of her. The conversation flooded back to her all at once.

Josh's breath had been harsh in her ear. "I don't have a condom here. We have to wait."

"Fuck it," she'd said. "No one gets pregnant the first time they try." Then she'd kissed him roughly, and he'd groaned into her mouth, his hands caressing her, his hard body pressing against her. Fire, she was on fire for the man she loved more every day.

He broke the kiss, breathing hard, his forehead resting on hers. "It can happen. How you think I got so many siblings so fast?"

She undid his jeans, sliding her hand in to hold his throbbing hard length. "Please, Josh, I need you so badly." She'd been away for a week at a bridal expo and had missed him so much. Then she'd freed him, spread her legs, and guided him right where she wanted him.

He took her in one hard thrust and then stilled, deep inside her, cradling her face with one big hand. He spoke between kisses. "It's fine." *Kiss.* "We're getting married next month." *Kiss. Thrust.* "And we both want kids."

"Yes," she breathed.

He pulled almost all the way out and slid back in. "Hailey," he said on a groan.

She sank her teeth into his lower lip. His response was immediate, surging within her, his hand fisting in her hair.

He pounded into her. Again and again and again.

Everything in her coiled hot and tight.

Yes, yes, yes.

Their gazes locked and the intensity ratcheted up as his hand slid under her hip, tilting her at just the right angle as he thrust. She gasped, her nails digging into his shoulders, hanging on for a wild exhilarating ride.

Hot. Hard. Rough.

No holding back.

Need like she'd never felt before clawed at her. She greedily took all he gave, her body clenching around him with every deep thrust. On and on and on, higher and higher. Her breath caught as her release slammed into her, a shockwave of pleasure so powerful her vision dimmed. She panted, her heart pounding in her ears, as he took her further, more pleasure arcing through her with every hard thrust, and then she went over again, a soft cry ripping from her throat. His breath was harsh in her ear as he pumped into her for his own release and let go with a long guttural groan.

He gave her his weight; their bodies slick with sweat, joined in a way they'd never been before, no barrier between them. She held him tight to her, overwhelmed with all she felt for him.

She blinked, flushed with the hot memory, and focused on him again. "I remember."

He pulled her upright and stroked her hair back from her face. "We haven't stopped having sex since then. You've been all over me for weeks, no break."

She pouted. "You wanted a break from me?"

He nipped her lower lip. "I fucking loved it. I'm making a point. After that time here, I used a condom, but I'm starting to think maybe I didn't need to. You've been emotional, crying at the drop of a hat, and I counted and I think we have to consider the possibility—"

"Are you saying I'm pregnant?" She'd forgotten to track her cycle with all the wedding stuff.

"It's possible."

She shoved his hands away. "I can't be accidentally pregnant! *I* was an accidental pregnancy. I would never allow that to happen."

Josh just looked at her, waiting patiently in his solid, stable way.

She folded her hands in her lap and stared at them, saying quietly, "I allowed that to happen."

He sat next to her and took her hand. "It's not like it was when you were the surprise pregnancy. You and I are about to be married. We said we were going to start trying on the honeymoon. You know I want kids. I can't wait and, if it's true, it'll be the best wedding present you could give me."

Her lower lip wobbled. "I can't be a pregnant bride!"

"No one would know. You won't show by then." He cupped her jaw and turned her toward him. "I love you so damn much. Nothing would make me happier than to have a family with you. That's why I let you have your way with me on our engagement anniversary." He kissed her. "Be happy with me on this."

"I am happy," she said, tears leaking out. "You'll be a great dad. You're so wonderful." She broke down in tears.

Josh pulled her close for a moment, her head pressed against his chest. Then he kissed the top of her head and stood, walking around to the other side of his desk.

She wiped her tears and took a moment of deep breathing to compose herself before announcing, "And in other news, I have no wedding gown." She stared straight ahead, fighting to remain calm. "But it's okay. There always has to be one thing that goes wrong with a wedding, and it's best to get it out of the way. So I'll just quickly find another one-of-a-kind designer original in my size in only two weeks and everything will…" She trailed off as Josh placed a plastic bag in her hand. She opened it and found a bright pink box. A pregnancy test. She swallowed hard.

"I picked it up today," he said gently. "It says to do the test in the morning, so do it tomorrow morning and we'll go from there, okay?"

She bit her lip and nodded.

He held her by the chin. "And don't worry about the gown, okay? I'll make sure you have one and protect it with my life."

She blinked back tears. He was a protector—for her, for all of his younger siblings, for his country for years in the army. He was a fierce warrior and she was his partner, his equal. He always said that about her, and she loved that he thought of her like that, especially the warrior part. She summoned that fighting spirit to battle back the tears. "Okay, thank you. And I will make sure the wedding goes off perfectly."

He nipped her lower lip. "I don't need perfect. I just need you."

She twisted her lips to the side. "Are you saying I'm not perfect?" Ha. Add another flaw to the list—she'd accidentally made him get her pregnant. Maybe.

His dark eyes danced with amusement. "You're as perfect as I am."

She found herself smiling, which astounded her given the shocking turn of events. "What if I am pregnant?"

"Then I will be the happiest man on earth."

She beamed a smile at him. "I'll be happy too. I'll need to do a lot of planning though, buy all the latest parenting books. I know nothing about being a mom."

"Are you kidding?" He gestured over to Max and Rose, their fur babies happily lying side by side, holding their chew toys close. "Look how good you are with them. They're happy and well-adjusted."

She laughed. "I'm sure it's just the same thing."

He wrapped her in his arms. "And you're amazing with Owen. You're a natural." Owen was their six-month-old nephew. A beautiful baby with blond tufts of hair that stood straight up like duck down and two little pearly baby teeth on the bottom. He was Claire and Jake's son. Jake was Josh's identical twin, so they all spent a lot of time together.

"You're great with him too."

He gave her a small smile. "Thanks. I helped raise my younger siblings. Mad was only one when our mom left."

She cupped his stubbled cheek. "I know. She was lucky to have you."

His dark eyes were intent on hers. "We're ready for this."

"We are."

He grinned. "I was practically dancing at the drugstore just at the thought of it."

Her eyes widened. "You? Dancing?"

"I know. Hard to believe. I almost did a jig."

She burst out laughing. Josh was so not a dancer, though he did do a nice waltz. He'd learned it purely for seduction reasons, he'd confessed to her once. It totally worked.

2

The next morning she met Josh in their bedroom and held up the pregnancy test stick.

Josh stared at it, let out a victory whoop, grabbed her, and spun her around in a dizzy happy dance. They were pregnant.

She'd thought she'd be scared or shocked, but all she felt was pure happiness. Hard not to feel jubilant with Josh beaming at her with the biggest smile she'd ever seen on his handsome face. She pulled away to set the test on the nightstand and turned back to him, her own smile so big her cheeks hurt. Everything seemed bright and light and so right.

Josh threw his arms wide. "Congratulations, new mom!"

She threw her arms wide too. "Congratulations, new dad!"

They laughed, and then he grabbed her and hugged her again.

She wrapped her arms around him, sure it would be smooth sailing from here on out. Look out, world! Here comes the pregnant bride for the wedding of the century! With Josh by her side, nothing could get her down.

Uh-oh.

She pulled away, ran to the bathroom, and threw up. Morning sickness. Right on time.

Mission wedding, get 'er done. There was nothing Josh would deny his bride. Not even a destination wedding at the royal kingdom of his former rival, Prince Phillip Rourke, the playboy prince. Never mind that Josh was a casual guy who would've been happy with a courthouse ceremony followed by celebratory drinks at his bar. When Hailey had said yes to his proposal, tying her life to his forever, he'd made her a promise—to always look out for her happiness. And he never broke a promise.

He wasn't one of those sappy whipped men at their woman's beck and call. No, sir. He was simply a man of honor. Truth was, when he finally did fall for Hailey, he fell *hard*. For a while there, he'd thought he might be losing his mind, but now things were on an even keel, where he liked them. He and Hailey were partners and deeply in love. She'd do anything for him and vice versa. She already did so much, fussing over him at home and at work, bringing softness to his rough and gruff. She even left little love notes around the apartment for him to discover. Naturally he'd crack skulls to ensure her happiness. That was a no-brainer.

So the day after Hailey came to him with the wedding gown problem, he'd parked his ass in that uppity bridal boutique with his pregnant teary bride until he was sure the job would be done on time and to Hailey's satisfaction. Did he secretly bribe the designer to work overtime with a promise of future work for his famous sister-in-law Claire Jordan? Maybe. Did he charm the worker bees? Definitely. Did he scare away a few patrons to neutralize the threat to mission wedding gown? Damn right. His bride wanted a designer original and that was exactly what she'd get. No time for beadwork, but whatever. When she tried on the dress the day before they were scheduled to leave, it was beautiful and Hailey was happy. Mission accomplished.

Hailey was doing fantastic now, much calmer about the wedding as her focus shifted to the baby growing inside her. The men in his family had strong swimmers. He'd been fairly certain he'd get her pregnant quick. He loved seeing her glowing and happy, talking to her belly on a regular basis as she filled the little one in on the world. The wedding was almost here, only two days away. They'd just spent several days enjoying Paris, gorgeous in the June sunshine. He loved seeing the city through Hailey's wide blue eyes. She was a romantic at heart and Paris was everything she'd hoped. It had been especially nice to enjoy the time with her without their constant furry companions, Rose and Max. Claire and Jake would be bringing them later by private jet, along with Hailey's wedding gown.

Now they were on the ferry to Villroy Island. He looked over as Hailey came up from the lower enclosed deck, where she'd spent a good amount of time in the ladies' room. She was seasick and morning sick. Her face was pale and strained, her lips drawn into a grimace, strands of her strawberry blond hair whipping in the wind, most of her long hair in a scraggly ponytail. And she'd never looked more beautiful, his pregnant bride.

He closed the distance, wrapping an arm around her shoulders and guiding her to the rail. "You okay?" He'd mostly stayed on top of the morning sickness, keeping her supplied with crackers and French baguette pieces, but the ferry's motion had proven too much. The ferry ride was close to two hours.

"I feel like I'm going to barf up a lung." She hung her head over the rail. "Honestly, I have nothing left in me."

He rubbed her back. "We're almost there. Half an hour more. Come on, it's best to keep your eyes on the horizon." He guided her to a bench seat, and they stared at the choppy ocean and sky. He pulled a bottled water from his backpack and handed it to her.

She pushed it away. "I can't. I'm too nauseous."

"Just small sips." He tucked a stray lock of hair behind her ear and whispered, "It's not good for the baby if you dehydrate." They were keeping the baby news quiet until after the wedding. She was nine weeks along, according to the doctor, and not showing yet. In any case, the doctor had said hydration was important with her morning sickness and traveling.

Hailey dutifully took a sip of water. She was a trooper. "I can't wait to get off this boat. I just want to brush my teeth, get into pajamas, and curl up in bed."

"It's afternoon."

She stared at the horizon, holding herself very straight and still. "I'm exhausted. You try heaving for hours while a baby sucks what little energy you have left out of you."

He cupped her head and kissed her cheek. "My warrior princess, you got this."

She took another sip of water, grabbed his hand, and squeezed. She loved him. He got the message every day in every way—her affectionate gestures, her words, her smile full of warmth, her eyes full of love.

He stood to see if they were getting close. The island came into view. He and Hailey had been here last July for Princess Silvia's wedding. (The princess had had both a stateside and island wedding.) Villroy Island was untouched by modern times for the most part, though they did have cell phones and internet. The coastline was rugged with cliffs. Inlets with fine sand beaches nestled between the cliffs overlooking turquoise water. Port Axel was the main commercial base for fishermen, the traditional basis of the economy. The seafood was incredible—tuna, bass, monkfish, shellfish, and more. There was an old lighthouse with a red top, tons of white boats bobbing in the water, and nestled close to the port were white buildings with red roofs. Farther inland and along the road to the palace were cottages, white with blue trim. On the far side of the island were dunes and wetlands that they hadn't had time to explore.

And in the center of it all on a hill stood the royal palace, also called Amalie Palace. He knew the palace from the princess's wedding and the numerous pictures Hailey had referred to during her planning. It had once been a stone circular fortress in the time of the Vikings. That crumbling structure stood to one side and a newer palace had been built next to it. Fire had taken a few of those palaces, the current one built in the eighteenth century and renovated many times. Now it looked more like a fairy-tale castle. Made of sandstone with copper roofs, it reached five stories, six stories in the two towers, with multiple spires. Two long wings stretched on the sides, forming an enormous courtyard that opened onto manicured gardens. Most of the royal family lived there, except for Princess Silvia, who lived in America with her husband.

Half an hour later, the ferry finally docked, and he let out a breath of relief that Hailey had made it without getting sick. He stood again, surprised to see a huge crowd waiting at the dock—photographers and cameramen, along with a shit-ton of people holding up their phones to get pictures. There were also three black Mercedes with tinted windows that he knew belonged to the royal family; he'd ridden in one last time. His eye caught on a huge banner: Congratulations Josh and Hailey!

He quickly sat down next to Hailey. "They're giving us a royal welcome. It looks like the whole island showed up. Cameras, video, the works."

She gaped at him. "I didn't plan this part. There's supposed to be a welcome reception at the palace tomorrow. Look at me, I'm hideous!"

He winked. "Don't worry, I'm handsome as ever."

She laughed and then got serious. "What am I going to do?" She looked down at herself in a casual loose white tunic, pink leggings, and strappy tan sandals. "I'm not dressed for this."

He gestured to himself in a gray T-shirt, faded jeans, and sneakers.

"You always look like that. They're looking at me as a wedding planner. I have to set a professional tone." She was probably right, being the bride and the best wedding planner in the world, in his opinion. Maybe after this wedding, the world would agree with him.

He worked the hair band out of her scraggly ponytail and smoothed her hair down. "Just brush your hair out. The rest of you looks great. You never take a bad picture."

She grabbed her purse and headed to the lower deck. One of the crew members brought out their wheeled luggage. Josh arranged their backpacks on top.

Hailey emerged only a short while later, looking glossy and made-up right down to her pink glossy lips. She'd tied a sheer pink scarf around her neck, which made her outfit look dressier. Honestly, she could wear a sack and make it look good. He didn't think he'd ever get used to her beauty. She was a former beauty queen; the pageant winnings had helped put her through college.

She crossed to him. "What do you think? Am I picture ready? It'll probably be in the bridal magazines."

"I think you look stunning as always." He palmed her hand and gave her a ginger candy. They were supposed to help with nausea. "Suck on this."

She unwrapped the hard candy, a smile playing over her lips. She raised her brows suggestively. "Now where have I heard that before?"

He chuckled. "After you." She walked ahead of him on the gangplank, and he pulled their wheeled luggage behind.

They arrived on the dock, and Hailey smiled and waved enthusiastically at the warm welcome from the crowd. No one he recognized. Their friends and family must be waiting at the royal palace. He kept pace with her, giving the cameras a small smile, his focus half on her, half on their destination at the waiting cars.

Prince Phillip emerged from the back seat of the center car and strode toward them, bodyguards flanking him. He was a little shorter than Josh, fit, with casually rumpled dark brown hair, chiseled cheekbones only seen on male models, and a ready smile. He had a huge internet following as a royal hottie. Barf. Hailey used to say Phillip was her go-to fantasy and she pictured him when she read a "swoony romance." Josh made sure he imprinted himself on her so thoroughly she now had no need for fantasy lovers.

"Welcome to Villroy!" Phillip exclaimed with a wide smile.

Hailey sped up. "Phillip! So good to see you!"

Josh caught up to her just as Phillip went for the double kiss on both of Hailey's cheeks. He waited patiently. Not a jealous bone in his body now that Hailey was his.

Phillip offered him a hand. "Josh, good to see you again."

Josh shook his hand. "Quite a welcome."

Phillip smiled tightly. "News spreads fast." He smiled indulgently at Hailey. "How was the trip? How're Rose and Max?"

"Oh, they're wonderful, thanks. The trip was great. Josh and I really enjoyed Paris. Thank you again for that generous wedding gift."

Yup, Phil was so glad they'd agreed to be the first wedding here that he'd covered first-class airfare and the five-star hotel in Paris. He was a generous guy and loaded, though the island kingdom itself was faltering as young people left in droves for better work opportunities.

"My pleasure." Phillip gestured them over to the photographers. They stopped for pictures.

A reporter put a microphone in front of Hailey's face. "Any comment on the furries?"

"What?" Hailey asked, her brows scrunching together.

"No comment," Phillip said. His guards barricaded the press away from them.

They followed him into his Mercedes. The cars in front and back of them must've been for security. As soon as the door shut behind them, Hailey asked, "What did he mean furries?"

"Maybe he meant our ring bearer and flower girl," Josh said. Rose and Max would be the flower girl and ring bearer respectively. Not like he didn't have a four-year-old niece, his brother Alex's daughter, Viv, who could've been flower girl. And his brother Ty's son, T.J., maybe could've been ring bearer with some assistance (he was eighteen months old and already running). Probably just as well that Hailey wanted their fur babies closely involved. Viv was a wild card and had run up, down, and sideways through the church aisle during her last time as a flower girl for Alex and Lauren's wedding. And T.J. was a typical Campbell kid, basically hell on wheels.

He checked that Hailey had a seat belt in the middle seat, pulled it from under her, and handed it to her. "You have to admit they're a little unusual."

Hailey did her seat belt and turned to Phillip, who was awfully quiet.

Josh narrowed his eyes at Phillip, an uneasy feeling coursing through him. "Problem?"

Phillip swallowed visibly. "There's been a small mix-up, but I'm sure once we're all settled in and have a nice sit-down—"

"What is it?" he and Hailey asked in unison.

Phillip grimaced. "It would seem our new wedding planner has double-booked the venue."

"Double-booked?" Hailey echoed. "But we're the inaugural wedding."

"What is it, a dog wedding?" he asked since they were talking about furries. "Kick them out."

Phillip jammed a hand in his hair. "They're not dogs. They're people who refer to themselves as furries. They enjoy dressing in stuffed-animal suits." He cleared his throat. "There's a good number of them who came all the way from Australia. I'm afraid we can't get rid of them. They're quite entrenched and paid twice our fee for the privilege. I thought they would be here next week, but the wedding planner entered the dates wrong. I'm sure we can work something out for Saturday."

Hailey turned to him, her pale blue eyes wide in alarm.

Josh spoke through his teeth. "I will fix this."

"Lord knows I've tried," Phillip said.

And that was the difference between a prince and an ex-soldier. Josh would get the job done. On his watch, Hailey's dream wedding would come true.

3

This was a living nightmare! Hailey would've cried if she wasn't so horrified. Wasn't it enough that she'd battled nausea for hours just to get here? Now she couldn't relax at all. She had to power through on her queasy stomach. How could this even happen? She hadn't known Phillip had already hired a wedding planner for Villroy. Why in the world had he done that? Hailey's wedding was the inaugural wedding, and she was her own wedding planner. Would it have been easier for her to have her wedding at Ludbury House in Clover Park, where she worked? Of course! But after having the honor of planning Princess Silvia's stateside wedding to an American, business had poured in. It only made sense to agree to have her wedding on Villroy Island after all the royal family had done for her.

Phillip had gotten ahead of himself. Maybe he assumed her wedding would be so fabulous that the venue would take off. But Hailey never counted her brides before they were hitched. Grrr...

Josh was ramrod straight, walking by her side along the long path to the palace entrance. He was more of a laid-back ambler, so he must be furious too. He'd raise hell on her behalf, but that wasn't always the best way to get things done, especially where bridal things were concerned.

Emotions ran high over such a big occasion. It took finesse, it took tact, it took—

She gasped. The guards had just opened the palace doors, and right there in the beautiful two-story white marble great hall with gilded mirrors and beautiful silk damask wallpaper the color of the sea shot through with gold leaf pattern—a kangaroo hopped by.

Wearing a bridal veil.

A koala in a top hat chased her.

Her face flushed hot, her hands in fists. She wanted to hurl obscenities at the kangaroo-koala couple usurping her wedding, kick them in their fluffy asses, and right out the door. But no. She would not stoop to that level because—She. Was. A. Classy. Lady. Also, the reporter from *Luxury Weddings* was due any moment.

A butler in a black suit and two footmen in the servants' uniform of white shirts with black pants approached, but all Hailey could focus on was a tall purple bunny chatting on his cell phone. She knew it was a man because his hand was exposed and it was large and hairy. He was leaning against the wall, his arm draped casually over a short wombat. She was pretty sure it was a wombat, all furry, cute, and cuddly. She ground her teeth. This could *not* be happening.

Josh moved swiftly ahead, speaking in a low tone to Phillip. Their luggage had already been taken care of by the footmen. She moved to catch up to Josh when someone bumped into her from behind. She yelped, nearly tripping on the smooth marble, but caught herself.

It was a tall tan dog walking on its hind legs. Maybe a dingo? "Sorry!" the feminine voice exclaimed from inside the furry costume.

Josh was there in a flash, glowering at the dingo, who scurried away. Hailey stared at the furry costume, the wedding planner in her quickly switching to logistics. It was only a temperate seventy degrees today, but by Saturday it was supposed to hit eighty, and those costumes would surely roast the furries. Ha! Roasted furries. Maybe she'd put that on the reception menu.

Josh slid an arm around her shoulders, guiding her toward Phillip. "I'll fix this," he bit out through a clenched jaw.

She looked up at Josh and whispered, "This is my area of expertise. Let me do the talking."

He grunted, which was not an agreement.

"Kicking ass doesn't work with brides," she informed him, keeping her voice low.

Another grunt. Great. Now she was going to have to get him to stand down so she could do her job. She was the wedding planner, and hadn't she powered through numerous hiccups with emotional brides and pulled off the perfect wedding every time?

Phillip gestured for them to follow down a long hallway to the right. Hailey might've appreciated the hallway with its wood paneling, frosted windows, and intricate ceiling of plaster designs framing gorgeous paintings if it weren't for a pack of dingoes chatting on one side, drinking beer and laughing like hyenas. Unbelievable!

She marched down the hallway. This was more than a hiccup. And this bride was past emotional to white-hot rage. Who the hell was this wedding planner who stupidly double-booked a wedding? It was the most basic thing getting the dates right. Hailey's wedding had been planned for a year. Well, the venue had been planned for almost a year, but still. This wasn't even a venue until she'd booked it. And what was with these furries? Why couldn't they get married at home in their natural habitat? She hadn't missed they were all native Australian species. The purple bunny being the oddball exception.

Phillip turned into a room at the far end of the hallway, and they followed him in.

A petite woman with shoulder-length brown hair was leaning over a large mahogany desk, giving the woman on the other side of the desk hell. It was her bestie, Mad Shaw. She'd recognize her badass stance and barking voice anywhere. "You're not fit to call yourself a wedding planner! You can't even kiss the toe of the best wedding planner in the world, who happens to be my best friend and the bride! You will fix this or you will never work on a wedding again!"

The young woman across the desk with long red hair and wide blue eyes leaned as far back in her seat as possible. Strangely, the woman could've passed for Hailey's sister, though with more freckles. Hailey was an only child.

Hailey flung her arms wide to the woman raging on her behalf. "Mad! My matron of honor to the rescue!" Mad was the youngest and only girl raised with a slew of big brothers. Josh being one of them. Soon they'd be sisters by marriage.

Mad whirled; her cheeks flushed red with exertion. She shook her head. "I showed up this morning to this disaster of an event. You know I got your back."

Josh chuckled. "Kicking ass and taking names as usual."

Hailey moved forward, arms still wide. "Get over here and hug me, lady!"

Mad closed the distance and hugged her. She pulled back. "I am beyond pissed. Your wedding takes priority and that is it."

Hailey inclined her head and crossed to the woman at the desk, offering her hand. "Hi, I'm Hailey Adams, also a wedding planner. I'm here for my wedding."

The woman shook her hand with a clammy limp grip. "I'm Bonnie." She had a slight lilting French accent. "Can you call off your matron of honor? She threatened to rip my eyeballs out."

Hailey waved a hand airily. "Don't worry about that." She took a seat at the desk, feeling Josh's gaze on her. The door to the room clicked shut. She glanced over her shoulder. No one had left the room. The silence was thick with tension from her barely restrained champion supporters. She turned back to Bonnie. "So it seems we have a scheduling problem. I'm supposed to be married at four p.m. in the chapel followed by a reception in the grand ballroom. When did you schedule the fur—" She stopped herself, correcting course to be civil. "The other wedding?"

Bonnie folded her hands tightly on the desk. "I'm afraid it's for the same time, reception to follow in the grand ballroom. Their costumes can be hot and they specifically asked for the early evening time. I'm so sorry for the mix-up, but they flew here all the way from Australia, paid double the fee up front, and I didn't realize the mistake until they'd arrived last night. You see, they wouldn't be accepted at home for their furry selves, and it was important they be recognized in marriage by the creatures they identify with." She lowered her voice conspiratorially. "The bride is pregnant. *Very* pregnant. I think that might be why she chose to be a kangaroo with a big pouch."

Hailey straightened her spine as Josh's hand landed on her shoulder and squeezed. She looked up at him, silently communicating that they would *not* be playing the pregnancy card. She turned back to Bonnie. "Be that as it may, my wedding must remain at the agreed-upon time. I've arranged for both *Luxury Weddings* and *Bride Special* to be in attendance. They'll be reporting on Villroy as a destination wedding and my wedding as the inaugural wedding. They didn't come here to report on a kangaroo bride. They came here to report on the wedding planner responsible for Princess Silvia Rourke's wedding in America. You see how it would be advantageous to Villroy's new venture and to your future employment to reschedule the other wedding?"

"Yeah!" Mad chimed in. "Your ass will be fired! Tell her, Phillip!"

Phillip approached, standing awkwardly next to the desk. "I'm sure we can work something out. It was an honest mistake, and Bonnie was the best applicant for the job."

"How many people applied?" Josh asked drily.

Phillip bristled. "Trust me, she was the only one close to qualified. She used to manage the fishing vessel scheduling at the port."

"She sucks at scheduling!" Mad barked.

Phillip turned to Hailey. "She's already got three weddings scheduled after this weekend, and we anticipate many more with the bridal magazines reporting."

Hailey spoke through her teeth. "If the magazines

discover this huge mistake, it would scare away business. Big time."

Bonnie piped up. "I'm so very sorry. Let's please work this out. Maybe we could shift your wedding to later in the day?"

Hailey closed her eyes, reaching for calm, trying to think it through. She couldn't even request her wedding be shifted to tomorrow because her mom and Josh's dad were set to arrive tomorrow afternoon. She couldn't chance them missing it if there were travel delays. So the question was: did she want to go on Saturday before a furry wedding and have to possibly cut the reception short to accommodate the other party, or go later and enjoy the ballroom as long as she could? She and Josh were leaving on Sunday for their honeymoon. "I'll take the later time."

"No," Mad protested. "Don't give in to her. It's her stupid fault. She has to make it right. You get what you want, end of story."

Josh leaned down to her ear. "Are you okay with this or being polite? Say the word."

He meant *say the word and I will raise hell*. But she had to think ahead to what was best for both the wedding and the venue. She was here to help Villroy and her royal friends. Plus the magazine coverage would be fantastic for the good of her future wedding planning business.

She smiled up at Josh. "I'm good." She turned to Bonnie. "My wedding will be at seven p.m. in the chapel, reception to follow as planned in the ballroom for as long as we want. Please add extra candelabras to the chapel and extra lighting to the ballroom to maximize photo opportunities. Let the other wedding party know they will need to end their reception promptly at seven to leave time for cleaning and setup for mine. I will personally supervise all the changes." She pasted on a smile. "I'm sure there's a lot I could teach you as a wedding planner, since you're new at it, which will ensure all future weddings on Villroy will go through without a hitch."

"Of course," Bonnie murmured, lowering her gaze to her desk.

Phillip clapped his hands together. "Excellent. I knew we

could work something out. Thank you, Hailey, for your understanding." He smiled. "Now let's get you settled in your room. I understand the *Luxury Weddings* reporter is waiting in the audience chamber in the west wing. No rush. They've been offered tea, and I believe she and the photographer are quite happy chatting with your sister-in-law Claire. I'll join them straight after this. Meet us when you're ready."

Hailey mustered a smile. "Sounds good, Phillip, thank you. I would like to freshen up." She stood to go, a small sense of relief washing through her. Her wedding was back on track and Claire and Jake were here. That meant they had her gown, her fur babies, and her darling nephew, who never failed to make her smile. Things were looking up.

She was walking to the door with Josh when Bonnie spoke up. "One more thing. Your flowers didn't come in. The tulips? I've been waiting all day and I was almost afraid to mention it."

Hailey whirled. "Afraid to mention it? You don't hide things from the bride. How could the flowers not come in? They were ordered months ago! You should've followed up." Her voice choked. It was one thing too many.

Josh took her hand and gave it a squeeze, looking into her eyes with a silent message: *I got this.*

She nodded, her lips pressed tightly together. Her man would handle it. A pregnant bride could only take so much. The baby would feel stress hormones, and she had to do all she could to let her know that she was being born into a loving stable family. She secretly thought it was a girl.

Josh jerked his chin at Mad to take his place at Hailey's side. As soon as Mad reached her, Josh turned and ambled over to the desk to let Bonnie know how things were going to be.

The last thing she heard was Josh saying ominously, "I'll wait."

∼

Hailey settled into her third-floor room, a beautiful suite of two bedrooms with a sitting area filled with gorgeous walnut antiques trimmed in gold. Gleaming hardwood floors, enormous stone hearths, and large windows framed by deep blue velvet drapes overlooking the sea added to the elegance. The bed in the bedroom she decided they'd be sleeping in was a full four-poster canopy bed with drapes in a beige and brown link pattern that could fully enclose the bed. So cozy and private. She could see spending her wedding night there.

Her luggage was already here. She was digging in the large wheeled suitcase for her toiletry bag when a knock sounded at the wooden door. "Come in," she called.

A young woman with her dark hair pulled back in a bun, holding a pitcher of ice water, stepped into the room. "Hello, ma'am." She curtsied. "I'm Anna and I'll be helping you during your visit. I've brought you some water." She moved quickly to a round antique table by the window and poured Hailey a glass, setting the pitcher on a trivet.

"Hi. Thanks so much."

Anna turned and bobbed her head. "Would you like some fruit salad or perhaps something more substantial?"

"Fruit salad would be great, and could I also have a slice of dry toast?"

"Of course." She turned and left just as quickly as she'd arrived.

Hailey smiled to herself and went to the en suite bathroom. Wow! There was a huge soaking tub for two, along with a glass-enclosed shower with multiple jets. So tempting, but she didn't want to keep the *Luxury Weddings* reporter waiting too long. She was supposed to have dinner with the *Bride Special* reporter tonight.

She set her bag on the long marble counter with double sinks and brushed her teeth. She gagged a little, sensitive now to toothpaste and just about everything, really, and quickly rinsed her mouth. She put a hand to her belly. "Baby, I sure hope this morning sickness passes soon. I need to make sure you're getting all that yummy nutrition." The doctor had said the pregnancy was progressing nicely, and the baby was due

January 22. Josh and Jake also had a January birthday. This little one and Jake's son, Owen, would be a little over a year apart, which would be great for cousin playdates.

She freshened up her makeup and then, feeling tired, settled in the bed, pillows propped up behind her while she waited for Anna to return. She must've dozed off because she was surprised when she heard the door shutting and no Anna was in sight. The fruit salad and toast were on the table.

"Thank you!" she called.

Anna pushed the door back open and stepped inside. "I didn't want to wake you. Do you need anything else, ma'am?"

"No, thank you. Please call me Hailey."

Anna bobbed her head and left.

So weird to be waited on. Hailey had been doing things for herself from a very young age. She settled at the table and slowly ate the toast, staring out the window at a spectacular view of the sea, which she appreciated so much more on land. By the time she finished the toast and a second glass of water, she was feeling much better.

The door swung open and Josh strode in. He shut the door and took a quick look around before heading straight for her, a grim look on his face.

"How'd it go with the flowers?" she asked.

He took the seat across from her. "I don't think the wedding planner is going to last long."

She straightened, alarmed. "What happened?"

He lifted a palm. "I made her cry. I never make women cry, except for breakups, but that shouldn't count. I never made you cry, did I?"

During their long rocky frenemy history, she'd been mostly mad at him, sometimes exasperated, always entertained. She'd only cried once, but it hadn't been directly because of him. "Nope, but I'm a helluva warrior, so there's that." She smiled cheekily.

He leaned forward, snagged her by the back of the neck, and kissed her. "That you are." He leaned back in his seat. "She must be a wimp. I've managed a wait staff of mostly women for years. Not one tear. I've definitely yelled at Mad—"

"Josh." He clearly felt guilty, but she needed to know the deal. "What did you say to Bonnie?"

"I told her I'd wait while she got on the phone to the florist and either got our order here tomorrow morning on the first ferry out, which is completely reasonable, or she got our money back and then hired another florist."

"And?"

He snagged a strawberry from the fruit salad on the table. "So the original florist couldn't come through on time, and they said maybe they could do it on Saturday if they got another delivery from their supplier. I said, 'Unacceptable,' and Bonnie burst into tears." He chewed on the strawberry and looked at her like *can you believe it?*

She gave him a sympathetic look. He didn't like to stand by on tears. He liked to fix the problem as soon as possible because deep down he was too sensitive to sit idly by watching someone fall apart. "What'd you do then?"

He reached for another strawberry. "I handed her a tissue and said I'd wait."

Hailey bit back a smile. She could just picture that, sympathy but no backing down. "Did she stop crying?"

"No. She sobbed harder, blubbering in French and English, so I just waited her out." He chewed and swallowed. "Finally, she called another florist. Flowers will be here on the first ferry tomorrow morning."

Hailey brightened. "And did she get our money back from the first florist?"

He lifted one shoulder. "I dunno. I left. That's her problem. It'll come out of her funds, not ours."

She stood and crossed to him, wrapping her arms around him. He pushed his chair back and hauled her into his lap. "You rock!" she told him, beaming.

He grinned. "I know." He kissed her and slid a hand to her stomach. "How're you feeling?"

"Much better. I kept down some toast and I'm fully rehydrated."

"Good. You're going to need a strong stomach when you see what's downstairs. The place is crawling with furries. I swear they're multiplying. You know, even the minister is dressed in a wallaby costume?"

She laughed. It was either that or have a breakdown, and she had too much warrior in her to go that route.

He kissed her cheek. "We'd better get to the *audience chamber*." He said the last part in a deep ominous voice, making her smile. "Jake texted that he needs out of that room. They've been entertaining the reporter for a while now."

"Then we'll go." She stood. "Did Bonnie get us tulips?"

"She said she did, but she ordered in French, so I can't be sure."

"I guess I'll find out tomorrow." She had a very bad feeling about this. There was simply no time for last-minute substitutions if Bonnie screwed up again. Josh had done what he could.

They headed downstairs and made their way to the audience chamber, passing numerous dingoes and strolling musicians in tuxedos carrying didgeridoos. She avoided eye contact, needing to keep her cool for the reporter. Seriously, it was outrageous!

4

"Hi, everyone!" Hailey exclaimed as she entered the ornate audience chamber. The massive room was clearly meant to impress with an antique hand-carved double throne at one end. A center chandelier in gold and crystal shone over glossy inlaid hardwood floors. There was gold trim on absolutely everything—the picture frames of royal ancestors along the walls, the ceiling's ornate carved detail, and around a huge painting in the center inlaid panel of the ceiling that looked like it dated back to the Renaissance. Long deep blue velvet sofas and high-back wooden chairs with patterned cushions had been arranged in two seating areas, warming up the space.

A chorus of hellos from the group—the reporter, photographer, Claire, Jake, and Prince Phillip—were quickly drowned out by her beloved fur babies barking their heads off, racing toward her and Josh. She bent down and pulled them close. "Rose! Max! How're my babies?" Their tails wagged madly as they licked her face, just as thrilled with their reunion as she was. Josh dropped to his haunches next to her, ruffling Max's furry head, and both dogs leaped all over him too.

He scooped up the dogs and stood, heading over to the group. Phillip stood and waited for her to take a seat on the sofa. Josh waited, too, before sitting next to her and setting the dogs on the floor.

The reporter, Evelyn, looked to be in her thirties, her blond hair in a sophisticated twist, her makeup subtle, mostly highlighting her brown eyes, and her dress was a chic satin Armani in a brightly colored abstract pattern with an asymmetrical silhouette. Hailey knew her designers. Evelyn offered her hand from the adjacent chair and spoke in a clipped British accent. "Hailey, nice to meet you at last after all of our emails."

Hailey shook her hand. "Yes, so nice to meet you too, Evelyn. And this is the groom, Josh."

Josh shook her hand. "Nice to meet you."

Evelyn indicated the young woman sitting on the end of the sofa across from them, her dark brown hair also in a twist, wearing a white pants suit. "This is Lucy, our photographer. You might've seen her on the dock earlier at your arrival."

Hailey and Josh stood to shake Lucy's hand. Hailey smiled over at Claire and Jake and worked her way down the sofa to them, hugging them both at the same time, one arm around each of their shoulders. "I'm so happy to see you guys," she whispered. Baby Owen reached up from Jake's lap and yanked her hair. She leaned back, carefully untangling Owen's pudgy fingers. The boy had some grip. "And you too, Owen." She held her hair back with both hands and kissed his cheek with a squeaky pucker. His brown eyes went wide at the sound, making her smile.

She greeted Phillip too and returned to her seat while Josh shook everyone's hands, kissing Claire's cheek and ruffling Owen's hair before taking his place at her side.

"Shall we get started?" Evelyn asked, placing a small recorder on the side table next to her.

Claire stood. "We'll leave you to it. Owen is overdue for his nap. So nice to meet you all." She walked around the seating area, stopping behind Hailey to lean down and whisper, "Small issue with the rings, but I'm sure it'll be taken care of tomorrow. Just keep a close eye on the dogs."

Hailey's eyes widened. *What?*

Claire stared at the dogs, a grim expression on her face. "Check your texts." She walked away.

Jake joined Claire, holding Owen against his chest. "Nice meeting you all."

Phillip stood. "I, too, have some business to attend to."

"Was it something I said?" Josh quipped.

Everyone laughed and said their goodbyes. Except Hailey, who dug her phone out of her purse and turned it on. She'd had it shut off while traveling today. She stifled a gasp at Claire's text.

Do NOT freak out. The vet said the dogs should be fine. Jake let Owen hold the ring box when we first arrived in the room because he was fussy. Somehow he pried it open, the bands fell out, and Rose grabbed one. Max grabbed the other, and by the time we chased them down, they'd swallowed them. Check their poop and don't let them out of your sight.

Hailey's gut churned, nausea rising fast. "Excuse me." She bolted from the room, frantically searching for a bathroom. Finally she found a door that led outside and stood there, bent over, hands on her knees, waiting to see if she was going to throw up. When it didn't happen right away, she straightened and took a deep breath of bracing sea air. It was a gorgeous sunny day, not a cloud in the sky. So why did she feel like a dark cloud hung over this wedding? Like it was doomed—no, like it was cursed! First, the gown was ruined, then she had to power through with morning sickness, then the furry wedding, then the flowers, now the rings. She looked to the sky. *What else could go wrong?* She was afraid to find out. How could the one wedding that fell apart be hers? She'd never had so many disasters in all of her years as a wedding planner.

She sighed and walked back inside.

Josh strode toward her. "There you are. Are you okay? If you're not feeling well, we'll do the interview later."

She squared her shoulders and straightened her spine. "I'm okay. So here's the latest, Claire said the dogs swallowed our wedding bands. The vet thinks they'll come out the other end tomorrow."

He stared at her. "Seriously?"

"Why would I make that up?" she exclaimed. "Could this wedding be more screwed up? I swear it's cursed!"

He pulled her into his arms. "So dramatic," he murmured. "When you go big like this kind of wedding, there's bound to be some issues. It's a lot to bring together."

She pulled away. "I've planned plenty of weddings, including a royal wedding. This does not happen on my watch."

"Okay."

"What's that supposed to mean?"

He lifted one shoulder. "Obviously it is happening on your watch. It'll work out."

She gestured wildly. "What if it doesn't? What if it's a complete disaster captured forever in the pages of *Luxury Weddings* and *Bride Special*, making me look incompetent and unprofessional, and ruining Villroy as a wedding venue for all time, tanking the economy and destroying a royal kingdom?"

"No pressure."

"Exactly!"

He remained aggravatingly calm. "All that matters in the end is that we're married."

She threw her hands up. "That's not all that matters!"

He crossed his arms. "It is to me."

"Josh! How do you not get this? How can you be so calm when everything is falling apart?"

A feminine voice called to them. "Everything okay out here?" It was Evelyn. Shit. How much had she heard? She couldn't use stuff off-the-record, could she?

She glared at Josh for fighting with her in public like that.

He smirked, like *that was you, sweetheart*. They silently communicated all the time, but the pressure of doing that with a reporter witness made it much more intense. Hailey seethed.

He stroked her hair back and cupped her cheek, his gaze tender. He never minded their fights and rarely showed much temper. He'd even told her he liked her fighting spirit most of all. How could she stay mad at him when he so clearly loved her, flaws and all?

She gave him a small smile, took his hand, and turned toward Evelyn. "We were just heading back. I needed to find the ladies' room and I'm afraid I got lost."

Evelyn smiled and turned back toward the audience chamber, walking at a brisk pace. She and Josh walked slowly, a good distance behind. He lifted their joined hands and kissed her knuckles.

"Oh, Josh," she said on a long sigh.

"It'll work out."

She was having a very hard time believing that. "If you say so."

"It will. I'm going to make sure of it."

"What if we're cursed?" she whispered.

"Then I'll perform an exorcism."

"I don't think that works on curses."

He widened his eyes. "Magic?"

"Now you're being ridiculous. This is serious."

"You know curses aren't real, right? Just like luck isn't real. Life happens and you deal."

"I cannot believe you don't believe in those things. How plain your world is."

"Would you rather I be terrified of a curse and throw my hands up?"

"No," she admitted.

"Hailey, you go right on believing in your fairy tale and I'll make it come true."

A surge of affection made her stop, throw her arms around his neck, and kiss him. He returned the kiss passionately, and her world righted itself again.

When they broke apart, Lucy was standing there with her camera, smiling at them. "Evelyn told me you were on your way back, but you took so long. It's a great picture. Can I use it?"

Josh grabbed her hand and pulled her over to look at it. The kiss looked every bit as passionate from the outside as it had felt from the inside. Maybe even more so because Josh had this way of holding her, one hand cupping her head, the other arm around her waist, pulling her flush against his hard body. Why, they could be on the cover of one of her beloved romance novels!

Josh raised a brow at her in question.

"You can use it," she told Lucy. "And send me a copy. I'd like to frame that."

Josh grinned.

Once they were all settled back in the room, Evelyn said, "Everyone loves to hear the story of how the happy couple met. How was it for you two?"

Hailey glanced at Josh, who clamped his mouth shut. Thank God he was letting her tell her version. Frenemies who got out of hand was not the image she wanted to convey to the world. She turned to Evelyn. "We actually work just across the street from each other in Clover Park. I work out of Ludbury House for my wedding planning business, and Josh owns the Happy Endings bar. Over time, we grew closer. He took some cooking classes offered at night at Ludbury House, it's owned by the town and frequently hosts community events, and I met friends at his bar, so we talked quite a bit over two years or so, and we had a lot of connections that brought us in frequent contact at parties and special occasions. I'm close with his sister, his dad married my mom, and some of my friends are married to his brothers. He has a big family."

"Your dad married her mom?" Evelyn asked Josh.

"Yup." Josh didn't elaborate. He could be very reserved, especially with people he didn't know, and Hailey was immensely grateful in this instance.

"That's brilliant!" Evelyn exclaimed. "So you're actually her stepbrother."

Crap. Why had she said their parents were married? On the other hand, it would be obvious when their parents arrived tomorrow. Hailey resembled her mom, and all of the Campbell sons took after their dad. It was impossible to hide it, especially with how revoltingly lovey-dovey their parents were with each other.

Josh frowned, his voice sharp. "It's not like that. We found each other long before our parents got involved."

Evelyn beamed. "Your love was contagious. Mr. and Mrs. Second Generation! Love redux! No, Happy Ever After Redux!" She waved airily. "I'll think on the phrasing." She leaned forward. "I'd dearly love to interview them too."

Hailey shifted uneasily, not liking the direction this was going. Not only the weirdness of the stepbrother thing, her mom was the worst oversharer. She shuddered to think what might come out of her mouth. Probably something about how great Joe was in bed and the apple must not fall far from the tree. "They're not here yet. I'm not sure there will be time, but I'll run it by them." *There will definitely not be time.*

"I'd prefer to keep them out of it," Josh said.

Evelyn pressed on. "But our readers would love to hear how two generations have connected. Did you two help bring them together?" She winked. "A little matchmaking?"

"I'd prefer to keep them out of it," Josh repeated.

Hailey nodded once. "I think that's best. They're very private people. In any case, your readers might like to hear about our first date. Josh is a gourmet cook and he prepared a delicious steak dinner for me at his place." She leaned forward, sharing the best part. "He even prepared some steak for my little Rose." Rose popped up from the floor at her name and jumped onto Hailey's lap. Max leapt onto Josh's lap. She casually checked Rose's stomach, feeling for ring-shaped lumps.

Evelyn inclined her head. "Okay, so no parents." She wagged her finger. "Though I'm quite sure there's a story there. We'll circle back to that."

"We're done with that," Josh said in a voice that brooked no argument.

"Mmm," Evelyn murmured noncommittally. "So how's the wedding shaping up? I couldn't help but notice the abundance of wildlife in the palace."

"Damn furries," Josh muttered.

"It's no problem," Hailey chirped, sending Josh a stealth

please leave this to me look. He looked back at her brows raised like *what?*

She considered how to address the other wedding without throwing Bonnie under the bus. Phillip needed Bonnie at this early stage of building their client list. "It turns out there are two weddings on Saturday due to a mix-up. There were extenuating circumstances with the other wedding, but everything has been worked out. My wedding will be in the chapel at seven followed by the reception in the ballroom, until dawn if we want, though I confess I'll probably be in bed by midnight."

Josh squeezed her hand. "It is our wedding night."

Evelyn smiled. "So everything's right as rain? I heard there were a few hiccups."

Hailey stiffened. Had Evelyn overheard Hailey's freak-out in the hallway, or was everyone talking about this? There were a lot of servants around, who probably heard everything. Ugh. This was supposed to be the wedding of the century highlighted in all its glory in the glossy pages of *Luxury Weddings*, not the wedding from hell.

"I took care of the flower problem," Josh said. "Everything's fine."

Hailey chimed in as cheerfully as possible. "Flowers were slightly delayed. No problem at all."

"How is the gown?" Evelyn asked. "We'd love to get pictures of you in it ahead of time."

"It's here," Josh said.

Hailey smiled tightly. "Of course it's here. And I'd love to show you tomorrow."

Josh turned to her. "Well, it almost wasn't. I took care of the problem."

She narrowed her eyes at Josh, ordering him to stop mentioning problems. She turned to Evelyn. "The gown is just what was expected. It's quite stunning, an original design I'm sure your readers will drool over. I sure did and I know gowns."

"So everything's not falling apart?" Evelyn asked slyly.

Crap. She'd overheard Hailey earlier for sure.

"Nope," Josh said.

"Not at all," Hailey said, lying through her teeth. "Everything is working out just fine." If you substituted "fine" for one of Josh's pithy military lingo terms—FUBAR.

Josh put his arm around her shoulders, pulled her close, and kissed her cheek. "Couldn't be happier."

She softened, relaxing against him. "Yes."

The photographer, Lucy, leaned in. "Can I go to the bachelor and bachelorette parties tomorrow night to take pictures?"

"Of course," Hailey said.

"No," Josh said. One corner of his mouth lifted. "Sorry. Guys only." He didn't sound sorry at all.

"You're welcome to join us ladies," Hailey said. "You too, Evelyn."

"Wouldn't miss it," Evelyn said.

Hailey sent a silent prayer up that Mad's planned bachelorette party tomorrow night would go off without a hitch.

And the dinner with the *Bride Special* people tonight.

And the post-dinner visit with the king.

And the furries, the flowers, the rings, her gown…ahhh!

5

Hailey was immensely relieved to have a delightful seafood dinner with Josh that night, along with their family and friends, and the very same *Bride Special* reporter and photographer she'd previously worked with on their feature for Carrie and Zach's wedding. Now that had been a fantastic wedding! Seriously, Carrie had looked like a beautiful princess and Zach had been to die for as the besotted groom. Ludbury House had been filled to the gills with gorgeous flowers in a profusion of cheerful colors, and the reception had featured a live band and gourmet food. Hailey had been able to go all out because it was mostly funded by the magazine, who'd been there from proposal to vows.

Everyone had finished dinner, but they were lingering at the elegant long dining room table, chatting and sipping coffee or tea. Hailey was seated at the end, Josh next to her on her right, and the reporter from *Bride Special*, Judith, on her left. Prince Phillip had joined them, too, at the head of the table.

She sipped some water, her stomach happy for once, and took in her friends, who were like sisters. They were all married now, and she was very pleased to have helped them all find their romantic happy endings in a myriad of subtle ways. The kids were sitting at a small adjacent table. Alex and

Lauren's daughter, four-year-old Viv, was busy bossing eighteen-month-old T.J. around. T.J. was Ty and Charlotte's son. He remained oblivious to his cousin's bossing, happily pushing peas around on his plate. Jake had joined them, helping baby Owen sit at the table with his cousins. Owen was also playing with peas, squishing them flat on his placemat.

And there would be more babies soon! Hers, of course, though that was still a secret. Missy was six months along; she and Ben were expecting a girl. Lauren was in her eighth month; she and Alex planned to be surprised on the gender. And Carrie was seven months pregnant; she and Zach were expecting a boy. For sure, Hailey was in good company. She was thrilled her baby would grow up with such a fabulous extended family. Mad and Parker had been married almost a year now and were waiting to start a family, Ally and Ethan had been married almost a year too, and Sabrina and Logan had married four months ago. Babies were definitely in all of their futures. She let out a happy sigh. Maybe she'd start a kickass mom club soon.

The reporter, Judith, a woman in her fifties with a dark cap of hair, leaned close to Hailey. "I'm so pleased you invited us, Hailey."

"Of course! I'm thrilled you made time for us."

Judith smiled. "I knew this day was coming the moment I interviewed you and Josh together almost two years ago. The love was palpable in the air."

Josh grinned and winked at Hailey.

She smiled agreeably with the completely off-base statement. The truth was, back then she and Josh had been fighting like cats and dogs, not involved romantically at all. He'd stepped in as her fake boyfriend in his brother's place, said a bunch of nice things about her in front of Judith with a smirk on his face the entire time, and she'd been sure he was secretly teasing her. Now she knew he'd meant every word. Even back then, he'd respected her and her work.

"We've already got the headline," Judith said. "Queen of

the Happy-Ever-After Gets Her Happy Ending. What do you think?"

"I love it!" Hailey exclaimed. Her previous spotlight in the magazine as the wedding planner for Carrie and Zach's wedding had dubbed her Queen of the Happy-Ever-After (pulled directly from a compliment Josh had given her during the interview. Swoon!).

Josh smirked and tugged a lock of her hair. "She does love a happy ending."

She pursed her lips, shooting him a significant look because she knew exactly what he meant by that. *No sex talk in front of the reporter!*

He grinned, cupped the back of her neck, and pulled her close for a kiss.

"Are you getting this?" Judith barked at the photographer, Rob, sitting next to her.

Rob set his coffee down in a hurry and picked up his camera with the zoom lens. "Could you do it again?"

Josh had already sat back in his seat. He crooked his finger at her, wanting her to take the initiative this time. That finger of his could be so bossy! Still, she wouldn't deny him a kiss, especially in front of the *Bride Special* photographer.

She leaned close, cupped his jaw, clean-shaven for the occasion, and kissed him gently.

He squeezed the nape of her neck, keeping her close. "Barely felt that."

Their eyes met close-up. She was *not* going to make out with him in the royal dining room for the glossy pages of a magazine.

"I felt it," she whispered against his lips.

"That didn't count."

"That totally counted."

He smirked. "Do I need to do everything?"

"Shut up."

"Shut me up."

Her cheeks flushed hot. She kissed him like she meant it, a swift hard kiss. Then she pulled back and made a herculean effort not to glare at him. She was a loving bride with her besotted groom. *Warrior beast!* she silently hollered at him.

His lips curved up in a slow smile. "Love that fire."

She softened. He meant her fiery fighting spirit.

"See what I mean?" Judith asked Rob. "Lemme see. You got it, right?"

Rob showed her his digital camera screen, and they both looked pleased.

Judith lowered her voice. "So I heard there's been a change of plans. Your wedding was pushed back by a kangaroo wedding?"

Hailey spoke in her most professional tone. "I rearranged the time due to a scheduling mix-up with the new wedding planner here. She's still quite green, but I'm hoping after working with her tomorrow, she'll get up to speed. In any case, the other wedding will be completed long before mine, and everything will proceed as scheduled. I can't wait for you to see my gown for the photo shoot tomorrow."

"Those furries are hysterical," Rob said. "I got the best picture of the bride and groom feeding each other ice chips."

Hailey's brows shot up. "You're not featuring them too, are you?"

"It's priceless," Rob said.

Judith shook her head. "Your wedding is the feature. They'll be in a sidebar, probably only in the online version of the magazine. No worries! Just enjoy your special day."

Hailey nodded, her gut churning. Sharing the spotlight with a furry wedding was not her idea of a good image for her business or Villroy's new venture. What could she do? She couldn't very well demand they feature only her. This was all free publicity.

Judith asked them several more questions, probing about the proposal, the engagement party, and Hailey's wedding planning business. She answered as best she could, her mind stuck on the possibility of a kangaroo bride making Hailey's traditional wedding look absurd. She must've trailed off a few times because Josh jumped in, answering questions too.

Finally, everyone left the dining room. She and Josh were

due to have a brief visit with the king and queen, who wanted to welcome them.

Phillip joined them in the hallway. "This way to the private salon."

Josh crooked his arm and she took it, appreciating his manners on such an important occasion. She'd met the king and queen during her last visit at Princess Silvia's wedding very briefly, but still it was quite an honor to have a private audience with them.

"So slight change in plans," Phillip said with a grimace. "My father isn't up to a visit. He's been having some health issues and my mother is by his side. Gabriel will greet you in his place." Crown Prince Gabriel, heir to the throne, was much worse than Josh in the gruff and growly department.

"I'm sorry to hear it," Hailey said. "Is your dad very ill?"

Phillip's expression was uncharacteristically grim. "I'm not supposed to speak of it, but yes."

"So sorry," Hailey said.

"Me too," Josh said.

Phillip bowed his head. "Yes. Well. Thank you."

They walked in heavy silence until they reached the door of the private salon. Phillip put a hand on the doorknob and turned to them. "I should probably warn you Gabriel is furious about the furry wedding. He says it's an abomination to the royal tradition. He was barely on board with our destination-wedding idea in the first place."

She gulped. And then they were ushered inside.

Gabriel had his back to them. He wore a dark blue suit, his gaze fixed out the window at the sea.

Phillip went ahead. "Gabriel, Josh and Hailey are here."

Gabriel slowly turned from the window, a brandy snifter in hand. His features were so like Phillip's with dark brown hair and stunning blue-green eyes but not at all friendly—his eyes cool, sharp high cheekbones, full lips pressed together. His stance was regal, powerful, and proud. He'd been groomed to be king since birth and held himself accordingly. He said nothing, merely stood there, waiting for them to come to him.

Josh ambled over when she would've rushed, but her hand was still tucked in the crook of his arm, so she had to keep to his pace.

They stopped in front of Gabriel.

He stared down his nose at them.

Phillip gestured to her with a small head bob and bent at the waist.

She pulled her hand free from Josh's arm, bowed her head and curtsied. "Your Royal Highness, thank you for seeing us."

"Thank you for having us," Josh said. No bowed head, no polite deference to his title.

She elbowed Josh. He ignored her.

Gabriel stared at Josh, his expression even harder, jaw clenched tight.

Josh stared back, giving nothing more.

"Who would like a brandy?" Phillip asked in a cheerful voice.

"Nothing for me, thanks," Hailey whispered, becoming concerned at the staredown. "Um, Josh?"

He reluctantly turned from Gabriel. "I'm good, thanks."

Gabriel let out a sound of disgust and joined Phillip, helping himself to more brandy.

She whispered furiously to Josh, "You have to call him your highness. You have to show respect."

"He's just a man," Josh said.

"He is not just a man. He's soon to be king."

"A king is still a man who puts his pants on one leg at a time just like everyone else."

"Show some respect!" she hissed under her breath.

"I did."

She left Josh's side to try to smooth things over with Gabriel. The last thing she needed was to be kicked out of the royal palace two days before their wedding. She came up behind Gabriel and Phillip. The pair were having a fierce low conversation.

"Hello," she said, alerting them to her presence.

They stopped talking and turned to her.

She smiled at Gabriel. "Your Majesty, I just wanted to thank you for having us in your lovely home. It's quite an honor and one we don't take lightly. It's a dream come true for a bride, and I do hope that our wedding can assist Villroy with the destination-wedding business."

Gabriel's lip curled. "Our business is fishing."

Phillip spoke under his breath to his brother. "We agreed to give this a try. Don't be rude."

"Do not speak to me of rude," Gabriel snapped. "Swear to God, if it were up to me, that daft wedding planner and her furry lot would be dumped at sea."

"He doesn't mean you," Phillip quickly assured her.

Hailey lifted a hand and nodded.

Phillip scowled and turned to Gabriel. "There are major wedding magazines here. We will proceed as best we can."

"If it helps, I plan on supervising Bonnie tomorrow," Hailey offered. "I know you don't know me very well, Gabriel, Your Royal Highness, but I've run a very successful wedding planning business for six years now."

Josh's arm dropped over her shoulders. "She is the best. You won't find anyone better."

"We should've hired her," Gabriel told Phillip.

"No, you can't hire her," Josh said sharply. "We both own businesses back home. Her place is with me."

Gabriel merely raised a brow. Josh bristled at her side.

Phillip jumped in. "Bonnie reminded me of you, Hailey, with your similar coloring, and she was very enthusiastic at the interview. Now I'm afraid she's under pressure and may be cracking a bit."

Gabriel snorted and sipped his brandy.

"I will help put her back together," Hailey said. "I worked solo for years and there's quite a lot to keep track of. I'm positive both weddings will go off without a hitch."

Phillip smiled widely. "Hailey, I knew I was right to ask you to be the inaugural wedding. A toast to you." He grabbed a glass and filled it with a small amount of brandy, handing it to her.

Josh snatched it out of her hand, and Phillip went and poured another for her.

"Enjoy your brandy," Gabriel murmured. He set his empty glass on the long bar, turned, and left.

Phillip handed Hailey her glass. "Don't take him personally," he said in a low voice. "He does his duty, but he's not happy about it."

She glanced over at Gabriel's retreating back, tension apparent in every step. It must be hard to bear the kingdom on your shoulders, especially with an ailing father. As soon as the door shut behind him, she turned to Phillip. "No worries, really, I couldn't be happier to be here. I understand his point of view too. I'm sure you're all under quite a strain right now."

Phillip lifted his glass with a smile. "To Hailey, wedding planner extraordinaire, the best, most understanding bride, and our salvation!"

They all clinked glasses. Phillip took a healthy swallow of brandy. She and Josh held their drinks.

Phillip cocked his head. "You don't want to drink to that?"

"We did," Josh said straight-faced.

Phillip turned to her. "You did?"

Hailey nodded and smiled. "It was symbolic."

Phillip laughed. "I'll drink to that too."

Josh took her glass and emptied it into his before taking a sip.

"Would you like a different drink, Hailey?" Phillip asked. "I could ring for a servant to bring something else."

"I'd love some milk," she said.

Josh nodded approvingly.

"Okay, then." Phillip walked to the far end of the room, picked up a phone, and put in their order with the kitchen. He straightened, speaking urgently before hanging up and turning back to them.

"What's wrong?" she asked.

He walked slowly toward them. "The caterer's gone on strike."

Her stomach rolled and she slapped a hand over her mouth.

"Get the palace chef to sub in," Josh said.

Phillip shook his head. "Our chef refuses to cook for so many people after being snubbed in favor of outside caterers in the first place. I'm afraid he's very temperamental. Hailey, I'm so sorry. I'm not sure what to do."

Josh swore. "You should fire your useless chef."

"His family has served ours for generations. My hands are tied."

Josh rubbed the back of his neck. "Fine. I'll cook the reception food for our wedding. The furries can stuff it."

"No," Hailey said. "Josh, you have to do the groom thing. I don't want you working in a hot kitchen on our wedding day. You should be getting ready in your tux, spending time with your brothers, and I'm sure there will be lots of photos and reporter questions for you. This is our special day and—" her voice cracked "—we will enjoy it no matter what."

"I'll ask around through the locals," Phillip said. "See if we can find someone last minute."

Hailey looked to the ceiling, blinking rapidly. *No more hitches! No more!*

Josh turned to Phillip. "Time for us to turn in. It's been a long day. I'll be in touch tomorrow." He guided her out, speaking to her in a low soothing tone, but it wasn't enough to drown out the voice in her head. *This wedding is cursed!*

6

There were a lot of hitches on the way to getting hitched. It was now late Friday afternoon, approximately twenty-four hours before the wedding, and Josh hated to admit it, but his pregnant bride was falling apart right along with the wedding. He was partially responsible since he'd impregnated her and the hormones were surely messing with her head. Jake had said Claire had been snappish and a wee bit aggressive during her pregnancy. Hailey went the opposite route. She was currently in the bathtub, bawling her eyes out.

He paced their suite. Snappish and aggressive would've been so much easier to handle, but no. He got tears, which got him all riled up because they were much harder to fix, and her pain was his pain. So yeah. He was up to bat. He got it, he really did. She'd put so much work into the wedding and it had been one thing after another. When they'd arrived at the dock this morning to make sure the flowers arrived, it had been a raging disappointment to find not tulips, but mismatched wilting whatever they were. It looked like the flower shop had delivered every single bouquet they hadn't been able to sell and pawned it off on them.

He did an about-face and paced in the other direction. Max and Rose were curled up on the bed, ears perked toward the closed bathroom door.

"I know," he told them. "I'm trying. You two weren't much help."

On the walk back from the dock, the dogs had finally given up the rings. And while Hailey was happy the dogs wouldn't require surgery, she couldn't stomach actually using those rings. Kind of a shame, too, because he'd had them engraved. Hers said Warrior Princess, and his said Warrior Beast. That was what she liked to call him. In any case, Mad had taken the ferry back to France with her husband, Parker, this morning to buy two new gold bands. Not engraved. Whatever. Hailey would never know she'd missed out on that. He'd figured problem solved, but Hailey didn't bounce back like he'd hoped.

She'd taken her sour mood and tried to work through it by supervising everything being set up correctly for tomorrow. Bonnie wasn't appreciative of Hailey's interference with her job and let her know it. That didn't stop Hailey, and why should it? So far Bonnie had made a mess of things. Hailey insisted on helping while Bonnie just seemed to bumble everything, screwing up the most basic requests. Hailey had given him an earful back in the room, beside herself over the gross incompetence.

He'd backed her up, agreeing with everything she said in regard to Bonnie being an idiot. Hailey soldiered on through a welcome reception in the palace gardens, which included the locals. The furries showed up, too, helping themselves to the offered drinks and snacks. Josh couldn't even kick them out since the welcome reception was open to the public. Next Hailey went through a full photo shoot in her gown. No one cared about his tux and he was glad. There'd be plenty of pictures of them as a married couple, which was the important part.

She'd returned from the photo shoot and took to the tub in their private suite without a word, which was worrisome. She always had something to say. Then he'd heard the sobs.

He opened the bathroom door and poked his head in for the third time. "You okay?"

"Go away. I'm wallowing."

He shut the door behind him and went over to the huge soaking tub on a center platform with a surrounding ledge that doubled as a bench seat. He took a seat and tested the water, lukewarm. She'd started it only warm, not hot, mindful of her pregnancy, which she'd announced to the baby the moment she'd turned on the faucet. She was a planner and had already read a lot about pregnancy. Still, he needed to get her out soon before she went in the opposite direction and got a chill. "You've been in here a long time."

She flicked water at him. "I'm not up to talking. Everything is shit. Even the rings are shit. This is beyond awful. It's hideous. It's horrible. It's cursed!" More tears leaked out.

"Hailey."

"Go away."

He kicked off his shoes and slid into the tub with her, fully dressed, the water sloshing over the side of the tub.

She stopped crying and gaped at him. "Josh! Are you crazy?"

He grinned and maneuvered himself behind her, wrapping his arms around her waist. "You left me no choice. I can't just leave you in the tub all day."

"It hasn't been that long." She leaned her head back on his shoulder and sighed. "Woe is us."

He sank his teeth into the side of her neck and heard her sharp intake of breath. "You taste even more delicious now that you're pregnant." He kissed his way up her neck, gentler now. Sometimes she needed a little edge to get out of her head; sometimes a tender nuzzle to soften her up.

She turned to look at him over her shoulder. "Are you trying to sex me out of my mood?"

He held her by the jaw and nipped her lower lip. "Would it work?"

"No."

He spoke against her lips. "Well, let's see." She smiled. *Yes.* She turned in his arms and kissed him. He fisted his hand in her hair, claiming her mouth in a fierce possession, needing her soft and pliant, letting go of her worries. Her nails dug into his shoulders and she straddled him, pressing herself against him.

She tore her mouth away, tugging at his wet T-shirt. He helped her take it off him and set it dripping wet on the ledge of the tub. She leaned over the side and turned back to him. "There's a huge puddle."

"Later," he muttered, kissing her again.

She moaned in the back of her throat, her fingers sliding down his bare chest to the button on his jeans. It would take too much effort to peel off the soaking wet jeans. Besides, she needed this way more than him.

He broke the kiss, cupping the back of her neck, and whispered in her ear, "Leave it."

She struggled with the button. "No. I want you." He stilled her hand, and she looked up at him in clear frustration. "It's weird how much I want you since I'm pregnant. You'd think biology would've shut it down. Mission accomplished."

He smiled, loving when she picked up on some of his vocab. He often spoke of the mission. "Guess I'm irresistible. Let's get out of the tub."

"No. I can't wait."

She kissed him roughly, and he took over the kiss, the fire igniting between them. Fuck. He couldn't safely carry her out of the tub, both of them soaking wet with water sloshed all over the floor. She wanted it here, then he'd give it to her his way.

He broke the kiss. "Turn around. You know what I like." He lowered his voice to a guttural growl that always got her attention. "Tell me what you need to do."

Her pale blue eyes dilated, her lips parting. "Spread my legs and surrender."

"Yeah, sweetheart." He brushed his thumb over her bottom lip and jerked his chin at her. "Turn around for me."

She huffed. "Pulling out the sweet words just to make me agreeable."

He waited, biting back a smile.

She turned around as requested, leaning back against him

and spreading her legs. He didn't touch her until she lifted her arms, resting them over his shoulders.

His cock surged painfully against his jeans. "Beautiful," he growled in her ear, his hands cupping her breasts, brushing his fingers over the hard peaks. She arched her back, asking for more. He pinched her nipples and she cried out; then he soothed her with soft caresses. She relaxed against him. He rolled and tugged her nipples, sucking and nipping her neck, until she was writhing against him.

"Josh, please, I'm so turned on. Let me have you."

He cupped one breast, strumming her nipple while his other hand delved between her legs. She sucked in a breath, quiet now as he stroked up and down her. He wouldn't take her, only pleasure her. She needed to let go.

He made slow lazy circles that had her hips rising to meet him. With his other hand, he flipped the switch to open the drain on the tub.

"Josh!"

"Let's see if I can make you come before the water runs out."

She tried to turn around, but he kept her clamped in place, one hand between her legs, the other around her chest. "You tricked me into getting out of the tub."

He increased the pressure, circling in on pleasure central. "Maybe I just enjoy a challenge. Now lie back and take it."

She let out a shuddering sigh and relaxed against him again. He was seriously regretting wearing his jeans in the tub. He was about to bust the seams with his blue steeler.

He stroked his fingers down her throat and she tipped her head back, resting on his shoulder, her arms loose now at her sides, completely relaxed. He took his time bringing her through her pleasure in stages, listening to her breathing. Her breath always caught when she was close.

The water slowly drained.

Her hips rolled, her breath in short pants. Finally, her breath caught, and he shifted his hand away. She grabbed his wrist and shoved it back, but that wasn't the way this game worked. It was his command, his control, and she knew it.

When she released his hand and shifted her arms to her sides, giving him open access, he rewarded her with more. He took her close to the edge of release and pulled her back, over and over and over, making her crazed.

The water was nearly gone when he got her to begging, out of her mind, unaware of anything but his fingers. She whimpered mindlessly, her hips lifting, her back bowing. He wanted her so fucking bad, wanted to drive deep inside, but he held on. Her pleasure, her need, was what mattered. He was steering her away from the abyss and over to bliss. He drew on every ounce of willpower to see it through.

"Josh," she whispered. "Love."

She was close. The water was gone.

"You want to come now?" He stroked her more firmly and then gently again, drawing lazy circles.

"Yes, please, please, please."

He increased the pressure, stroking over and over as his fingers closed over her nipple in a hard pinch. She went off with a throaty cry, bucking against his fingers. He stayed with her, slowing it down, letting her soak in every last wave of pleasure until she collapsed against him.

"Thank you," she whispered.

He tugged her by the hair, turning her for his kiss. "You're welcome. Tub's empty."

She twisted, curling into his lap and resting her head against his shoulder. He reached for the towel she'd left on the ledge and covered her with it. Then he just held her, all of him alive and aware, filled with the need to protect her, to make good on his promise to safeguard her happiness. He'd never loved anyone the way he loved her. Fiercely. With every cell in his being.

He tightened his arms around her. "I love you so damn much."

No response.

He looked down at her, eyes closed, cheeks flushed, pink lips parted in sleep. At least he'd given her some peace. He kissed her hair and kept her close, where she belonged.

Hailey walked to the dock with her mom and Mad for her bachelorette party, feeling refreshed. Josh's bachelor party was on a rooftop garden only royalty had access to. Phillip had suggested it and wanted to be part of it too. She let out a happy sigh. She'd had a nice nap thanks to Josh, though the poor man had sat in wet jeans for way too long. She'd taken care of him just as soon as she was fully awake, bringing him to the bed for their last time making love as an engaged couple. She'd gotten a little emotional thinking about that, and Josh had been super tender with her, his dark eyes full of love, his touch reverent.

She turned to Mad once they arrived at the dock. "So what's the plan? Party at the dock? Did you get some royal strippers?"

Her mom clapped. "Ooh!" Her mom was fifty-one with the libido of a twentysomething. A fact Hailey wished she didn't know.

Mad's brown eyes gleamed. "Better! I got us a party boat!"

Hailey turned at the sound of her friends screaming to her from the back deck of a small white boat bobbing in the water a distance from the dock. There was an open captain's perch on top for steering it, a tiny enclosed cabin below it, and a small deck. That was it. She would surely barf up a lung on that thing. "Couldn't you have gotten a bigger boat? This one seems so unstable."

Mad waved to their friends. "It can hold fifteen people. We've got ten sisters from another mister, your mom, the captain, first mate, and those tagalong reporters and the girl photographer. Oh, and, of course, Frank. Come on!" Frank was Claire's bodyguard, a constant shadow, who rarely spoke. It occurred to Hailey that they probably should've included Rob, the male photographer from *Bride Special*, too, since it wasn't exactly ladies only at this point. Oh well.

"Isn't that seventeen people?" Hailey asked.

Mad waved that away. "So we'll throw a few people overboard when we need space. Ha-ha. Don't worry. It'll be cozy but fun."

Her mom rushed ahead, waving and calling to the women.

Hailey dug her heels in. "Mad, I can't. I get seasick." She couldn't tell her about her queasy pregnancy stomach. She and Josh had agreed to keep it secret until after the wedding. She didn't want the big story from the reporters to be Pregnant Bride Weds Just in Time!

Mad planted her hands on her hips. "It's not moving *that* much. It's anchored here. Come on, I got sushi and champagne, a keg, and some of that fancy French wine you love."

Hailey stared at the dock. Those were all off-limits to her now that she was pregnant. "Maybe we could shift the party back to land? There's a cute beach just around the corner." Sure, the sun was setting and it would likely be pitch black soon, but who cared?

Mad scowled and shoved a hand in her dark brown hair. "Did I screw it up? It's my first time as matron of honor. I just wanted it to be perfect. Is it the sushi? You're sick of fish, right?" She shook her head. "I should've thought of that. This place is all seafood all the time."

"No, Mad, it's great. Really. I'm sure it'll be a blast."

Mad lifted her brows over worried eyes. "You sure I didn't screw up?"

She hugged her. "Not at all. It'll be wonderful."

Mad blew out a breath. "Great. Let's go."

Hailey followed her down the gangplank, where a crew member helped her on board a rowboat. Her mom and Mad joined her, and they were rowed to the party boat, where the captain helped them on board.

Hailey stood on the deck of the unsteady party boat. "Hey, everyone!"

"Congratulations!" her friends shouted.

"Thank you!"

She was determined to make the best of it. After all, Missy, Lauren, and Carrie were pregnant too. She'd just have whatever they were having and pray she kept it down. Barfing bride was not how she wanted to be remembered in the many pictures she was sure her friends would take. Not to mention the *Luxury Weddings* photographer. Her stomach rolled at the thought.

She set her purse under the long wraparound bench seat, where her friends' purses were stashed. She looked around. Twinkling white lights decorated the captain's perch above. She waved and smiled at the captain and Frank up there. The captain gave her a hearty salute. Frank nodded almost imperceptibly, looking like a muscled no-nonsense badass. He was all about staying on guard for Claire.

A clothesline strung from a rail of the captain's perch to a hook below held several pairs of risqué panties. There was also a large inflatable banana on a stand for some reason, one folding chair decorated with streamers, and a couple of skinny tables with the food. Coolers were stashed underneath the tables. A very efficient use of the small space. The planner in her was impressed.

She turned to Mad. "Wow, I'm…" She trailed off as Mad took off her shirt to reveal another shirt underneath. And then the rest of her friends and her mom took off their shirts too, like a wave of T-shirt reveal. She slapped a hand over her mouth, her eyes hot. They all wore white T-shirts that read Happy Endings Book Club with a red heart in the center that had pages like a book. It was the romance book club she'd started that had brought them all together.

"You guys!" she exclaimed.

Mad signaled and they all turned. The backs read Get Your Happy Ending!

She squealed. "I love it!" She rushed over to her friends. "Group hug!" Everyone huddled close. She glanced over her shoulder. "You too, Mom!"

Her mom demurred. "I'm not a member of the club."

"You're family," Mad barked. Hailey's mom *had* married Mad's dad.

Her mom joined them, squeezing in next to Hailey, beaming at them. A moment later, her mom said, "Let's get a picture."

"Wait!" Mad pulled another shirt from a giant tote she'd stashed to the side and gave it to Hailey. "Put yours on."

Hailey put it on over her white dress.

Her mom spoke to Lucy, the photographer from *Luxury Weddings*, and gestured to them. A moment later, Lucy got a fun photo session going with them in a bunch of different poses.

After they'd finished, Mad told everyone, "There's matching Happy Endings Book Club mugs too. Everyone gets one as a parting gift filled with naughty party favors."

Hailey laughed. "That is awesome."

Ally piped up. "I'm dying to know what we're going to do with the inflatable banana." Ally was queen of the unconventional wedding and enjoyed the odd and unusual.

"Any guesses?" Mad asked.

The women answered in a chorus of replies—

"Blow job tutorial!"

"Get the banana in the hole!"

"Banana volleyball." That last one was from sweet Lauren. They all turned to Lauren, who blushed. "It is inflatable."

Ally laughed. "Omigod, Hailey, wouldn't a blow job tutorial be a great add-on for our business?"

"No!" Hailey said with a laugh. Imagine the press with that!

"It's banana ring toss," Mad said. "But don't worry, if you're looking for a penis, we have penis cake for dessert!"

Everyone laughed.

Mad gestured to the tables of food. "Okay, everyone, eat up, drink up; then it's on to games."

Hailey stuck to water and some plain crackers to be safe. She was especially glad she did when the wind picked up, rocking the boat so much they had to tuck the food into the coolers so it wouldn't tip off the tables. She tried keeping her eye on the horizon, but it was difficult to focus on with her friends pulling her in different directions. By the time they finished banana ring toss, guess-who-got-you-the-panties (not too tough for her to figure out, she knew her friends well), and moved to the last game, Hailey was just praying for any excuse to get back to land.

She found the first mate circling the deck, offering drinks. "Is there a ladies' room on board?"

"Yes, it's below deck. Fair warning, the boat rocks more below, so hang onto the rail."

She nodded and quickly went below, carefully making her way to the bathroom. Oh God, it smelled so bad in here. She threw up in the sink, quickly rinsed her mouth and the sink, and got out of there. She made her way back to the upper deck, where Mad promptly dragged her to a chair.

"Time for the next game," Mad said cheerfully. She stepped behind Hailey and tied a blindfold over her eyes.

"What kind of game is this?" she asked weakly. With her eyes covered, the boat's motion felt worse.

"We all got you a stylish accessory or piece of clothing," Mad said. "You have to put them on blindfolded while sitting in a chair, and then you can see the whole thing put together at the end. You'll love the stuff we got you. Claire was in on it."

That meant designer, possibly haute couture. She battled nausea and held her hand out. "How many pieces?"

"Ten! Here."

Hailey felt something lacy. "Tell me I'm not supposed to put on lingerie blindfolded."

Mad laughed. "Nope!"

She felt the lacy thing, giving it a tug. "It's stretchy."

"Try your head," Claire's throaty husky voice called out.

Headband. She slipped it on. "Next, hurry!" She didn't want to miss out on the cool stuff, but she didn't want to barf all over it either. She was sure Lucy was taking pictures, along with her friends.

"What's the hurry?" Mad asked, handing over something silky.

"It'll be funnier if I put it on in a hurry." She tied the silky thing around her neck. "Next!"

She moved as fast as she possibly could without standing,

putting everything around her head, neck, shoulders, and wrists while battling nausea. "Is that everything?"

The blindfold was ripped off. Mad grinned. "That's everything. Stand up and model it."

She stood, felt the telltale lurch of her stomach, the burn in her throat, and dashed for the rail, tossing her cookies into the sea. Then she just stood there, leaning over the rail and panting, hoping that was the last of it.

"Hailey," Mad said and knocked into her when the boat suddenly rocked.

Hailey tipped right over the rail and into the water. It happened so fast she didn't have time to yelp. One minute she was panting through nausea; the next she took a dunk.

She came up sputtering. *Are you fucking kidding me?* It was frigging cold, her clothes were heavy from being soaked with water, making treading water difficult, and Mad was laughing.

"Are you okay?" Mad called, still laughing.

Hailey smacked the water, furious after a long line of bridal things gone wrong. "You don't throw a pregnant woman overboard!"

"Oh my God, you're pregnant!" Mad hollered.

Everyone rushed the rail, gaping at her. Lucy snapped pictures.

The first mate tossed her a life preserver, and she kicked back to the boat and made her way up the ladder. Then she just stood on the deck, soaking wet and spitting mad.

"Are you really pregnant?" her mom asked, a hand to her throat.

"Yes, Mom, I really am," Hailey bit out. Like she would just go around telling everyone she was a pregnant bride when she wasn't.

"I need to sit down," her mom said in a shaky voice. She retreated to the bench seat and stared at Hailey. "I'm going to be a grandmother?"

Hailey wrung out her dress. Ruined. Everything was ruined. The reporters had gotten an earful, she'd let Josh down by blabbing their news when they'd said they'd wait, and now her mom was freaking out. "That's how it works, Mom."

"Congratulations!" Mad exclaimed.

Her mom smoothed her hair and looked up at Hailey. "How did I get to be so old?"

"That's right, Mom, it's a-a-all about you. No one worry about the pregnant bride with the wedding from hell!"

Dead silence. Everyone stared at her in shock.

Mad broke the silence. "Just because you fell overboard doesn't mean your wedding is ruined."

Hailey lifted both hands and ticked off on her fingers all the ways it had gone horribly wrong. "I'm on my second wedding gown! Furry wedding preempt! Flowers are shit! Rings are literally shit! Caterer is on strike! And now my secret is out. I'm the pregnant bride, everyone! There's your headline! The wedding planner's wedding is falling apart!" The absurdity of it hit her all at once and she just started laughing like a loon. "This wedding is cursed!"

The women spoke all at once.

"Someone call Josh."

"Get her back to shore!"

"Holy crap!"

Somehow Hailey got from point A—soaked and shivering on a party boat—to point B, tucked into bed in her pajamas. Claire commandeered her, though the details were fuzzy between the nausea, the chill, and the sinking despair of knowing not just the wedding was cursed, she was cursed. And her career was sunk right along with it. No one would ever hire her again after this disaster of a wedding.

7

Hailey woke the next morning, her wedding day, with a lingering sense of despair. She'd dreamt she was walking down the aisle, and right before she got to Josh, the floor opened up and she landed in the sea. Gee, wonder what inspired that dream. She reached blindly for Josh and felt only blanket. Then she reached some more. Still no Josh. She opened her eyes and propped up on her elbows. He wasn't in bed. Rose and Max were curled up at the foot of the bed.

"Josh?" she called.

Silence.

She sat up and grabbed her phone from her purse, powering it on. There was a text from Josh. *It's bad luck to see the bride on our wedding day before the vows. I'm helping Jake with Owen and hanging with my brothers. I already fed the dogs and took them for a walk. See you at the chapel. Love, Josh*

She tossed the phone on the bed. Sure, now he paid attention to wedding traditions. Now when she was wallowing in the pit of despair. She grabbed her phone again and sent out a group text to her friends. *Anyone around for breakfast? Lunch? Anything?*

The excuses started rolling in, all of them boiling down to: Busy with my own thing. See you at four for getting-ready time.

First Josh and then her friends ditched her. *Fine.* The pregnant cursed bride would spend her wedding day alone. No, not alone. She'd spend it with her fur babies. Only they understood her. She shifted to the end of the bed and stroked them both. Rose's ears perked, but they both kept right on napping. She sighed and headed to the bathroom to get ready. She really couldn't handle being alone today. And she couldn't handle even one more thing wedding related. She needed a break from all that.

That was when she remembered Anna, the nice woman who'd brought her fruit salad and ice water before. She picked up the room phone and called the kitchen, hoping to find Anna, and was transferred directly to her. "Hi, Anna, it's Hailey. Could you pack a picnic for the beach today?"

"Of course."

"Great! If you can find a beach umbrella and a couple of chairs too, that would be perfect. I'd love for you to join me."

"You would?"

"Yes. Everyone needs a day at the beach once in a while." In fact, she'd been sure she wouldn't have time to enjoy the beaches here with all the wedding stuff, but here she was with a wide-open schedule. "I'd be honored. Just give me an hour to get ready."

She could hear the smile in Anna's voice. "I'll meet you in the front hall."

"Excellent."

And that was how Hailey went from freak-out to chill out. It was a wonderfully relaxing day at the beach. Max and Rose frolicked in the waves, dipping their paws in and running all around. Hailey read a romance by one of her favorite authors, and Anna paged through a celebrity gossip magazine. Hailey even got a little nap in.

She walked back into the palace through a side entrance, carrying her fur babies cuddled against her chest, and ran into Jake wearing a tuxedo with the white silk handkerchief she'd ordered special for Josh peeking out of the breast pocket. Why was Jake wearing his twin's tuxedo jacket?

"Hey, sweetheart," he said, walking over to her at a slow pace.

She was immediately suspicious. Jake never called her sweetheart. He also never moved slowly. "Do not even *try* to pull a twin switcheroo on our wedding day. No, sir! I know Josh like the back of my hand and you are not him."

Jake grinned and kissed her cheek. "I'm glad you got the right twin to marry. I'm on furry duty. My job is to impersonate the irate groom and kick the furry party out of the ballroom on schedule. Your groom is getting ready with the guys, enjoying his last hours of freedom."

"Ha-ha and thank you."

He glanced at her stomach. "I hear congratulations are due."

She blushed. "Claire told you."

"Everyone knows. Women talk; men listen." *They do?*

She leaned close. "We wanted to keep it secret until after the wedding. Was Josh mad that I told?" She figured the twins had talked about it already. She hadn't seen or talked to Josh since before the bachelorette party.

Jake grimaced. "Actually, Claire called me last night after she got you to bed and told me what happened. I filled him in, and all he cared about was you going overboard. He was furious like I've never seen him before. I had to talk him down."

"Would've been nice if he'd checked on me."

Jake gave her hair a tug just like his twin. "He did. He went back to your room and you were already sleeping. He checked your forehead for fever and took your pulse."

Her eyes widened. "He did?" She'd slept right through it.

Jake grinned. "Yeah, and then he texted to let me know you were okay, so Mad could live. He got up early this morning because he's planning something for you."

Her heart squeezed. "He's so wonderful, isn't he?"

He shifted his head side to side. "Sure."

"He is!"

"All right, all right." He winked. "Claire's checking in

with the hairdresser and makeup artist right now. Enjoy your bride time."

"I will."

She headed up to her suite, feeling very Zen after her beach day relaxing. She set her exhausted fur babies on the bed and took another shower before heading to the dressing area at the end of the hallway to meet with her friends.

The moment she opened the door, conversation stopped. She spoke into the silence. "Hello, everyone! Have a good day? It seemed you were all quite busy."

The women all chimed in at once, assuring her they were great. A little too great.

She narrowed her eyes. "Is there something I should know about?"

Mad shook her head. "Not a damn thing. Come in and take a seat." She gestured to a deep-red cushioned high-back chair. "We have something for you before the styling stuff."

"Oh-kay," she said slowly, taking the offered seat. Her friends gathered in a semicircle around her. "What's this about?"

Mad wrung her hands together. "We all felt really bad the way your bachelorette party ended last night. Hailey, I'm so sorry I knocked you overboard. It was an accident. And I'm sorry I laughed. It's the kind of thing me and my brothers would laugh about, seeing someone get knocked on their ass, but it was inappropriate. I'm really, really sorry."

Hailey shook her head. "Mad, it's okay. I'm fine now. And I know how you and your brothers are. All is forgiven."

Claire spoke up. "We wanted last night's party to show just how much you mean to all of us and it didn't quite get the message across like we hoped, so we got you this to wish you all the best on your happy ending after you helped all of us to find ours." She handed Hailey a leather journal.

Hailey took it, beaming at her friends. It was true. She'd made sure every one of her friends found their happy ending, nudging and supporting them all the way. It was the whole reason she'd formed the Happy Endings Book Club in the first place, to bring people together. That and the wonderful joy of dishing on romance novels and the delicious book boyfriends they loved.

Hailey ran her fingers reverently over the leather embossed with the royal crest—a lion wearing a crown with the sea and a fish beneath.

"It's a special kind of journal used only by the royal family," Mad pointed out. "Phillip offered it as a keepsake, and we all got in on it too."

Hailey hugged it to her chest. "This is so nice."

"Open it!" Mad exclaimed.

She did. The pages were a beautiful cream, unlined, with a gorgeous thick texture. And right on the first page Phillip had taken the time to sign it.

Hailey,

Thank you for being our guinea pig. I know you'll emerge a swan.

Much appreciation,
Phillip

She looked up at her friends, smiling. "Thank you so much. I'll definitely treasure this."

"Keep going," Mad said.

She turned the page. Another note, this time from Claire.

Hailey,

You brought me a sisterhood of real friends at a time when I felt alone in a crowd. And you gave me a nudge (Ha! More like a shove!) to go on a blind date with Josh, who turned out to be Jake, the love of my life. I joined your Happy Endings Book Club and truly found my happy ending. Sisters <u>forever</u>. Long live romance and the happy ending!

Love,

Claire

Hailey's throat tightened. Claire had been at the peak of her movie star popularity when they'd first met her. They'd all been a little starstruck, actually, but she'd turned out to be so down-to-earth and fun. "Claire, thank you. I'm not sure how much credit I can take for the twin switcheroo. I had no idea they were going to do that."

Claire smiled, her hazel eyes twinkling with good humor. "The only reason they pulled a twin switch was because Josh wanted to go on the date with you. So it all comes back to you." She gave Hailey a hug. "I love you, lady. Now keep reading."

Hailey wiped at the wetness in her eyes. "You ladies are going to make me cry."

Mad gestured to a mini-fridge. "We got you covered with cold compresses and sliced cucumbers. You cry as much as you want as long as they're happy tears."

Hailey laughed. "Thanks, Mad. You're a great matron of honor."

Mad smoothed her hair self-consciously, blushing. "Thanks," she mumbled.

Hailey turned the page to Mad's scrawl of a note.

Hailey,

You're my first close woman friend and I know all the credit goes to you. You pushed to get to know me and welcomed me with open arms into the Happy Endings Book Club when others might have found me surly. Shocker, right? You made me feel comfortable for the first time with a group of women and that is a miracle all by itself, but then you also helped and encouraged me every step of the way to open Parker's eyes and show him I was a full-grown woman who could handle him, and not the fifteen-year-old mouthy twerp he remembered. Now we're married and I've never been happier.

You taught me to believe in myself and to believe in love. I can't imagine my life without you in it, and now I don't have to since you're marrying my brother. You're stuck with me for life! Welcome to the family.

Love,
Mad

The tears fell in earnest now. "Oh, Mad, you've done so much for me too. Get over here." Mad was the first friend who saw the person Hailey was on the inside. Never catty or judgmental, Mad had helped Hailey claim her own strength as a woman. She'd also taught her self-defense and had treated Hailey like part of her close-knit family from the beginning. Hailey sniffled and opened her arms to Mad, who gave her a fierce hug.

Mad pulled away, tears in her eyes too. "I'll get the tissues." She rushed over to the vanity table in the corner of the room, pulled out a tissue and wiped her eyes.

"Hello?" Hailey called. "Pregnant bride tears over here!"

Mad grabbed the box and offered it to Hailey, looking at the ceiling to hold back her tears. They fell anyway. Hailey snagged a tissue and delicately wiped under her eyes.

She turned the page for the next message. This one was from Charlotte, a personal trainer who had once been terribly jaded about men. She was married to Josh's younger brother Ty.

Hailey,

I may have been the worst candidate for matchmaking, but once you put the idea of Ty in my head, he barreled right into my heart. Your unwavering faith in love and constant support gave me the strength to open up to Ty, you, and our friends.

I will always be grateful for your part in getting me through the harrowing time when I was on bed rest with T.J. Your daily texts and phone calls reminded me I was not alone in this. I had you and my sisters to back me up. Moving the Happy Endings Book Club meetings to my bedroom kept me part of the group I needed more than ever. I'm thrilled to call you sister. I love you with all my heart. No, you're crying. God, I'm already bawling just writing this. I wish you the happiest of happy endings with Josh. You deserve it.

Love,
Charlotte

Hailey looked up. "Char—" Her voice choked. It had been a difficult time for all of them when Charlotte was on bed rest. Both Charlotte and the baby had been in a high-risk situation. Luckily, they'd both pulled through. T.J. was a healthy toddler now.

Charlotte kissed her cheek and then hugged her. "Love you, girl."

"Love you too," she managed.

Charlotte pulled away with a smile. "I'm so happy for you and Josh, both for the wedding and the baby."

The women chorused their agreement, swooping in to hug her. She stood, surrounded by her sisterhood. "Thank you," Hailey choked out. She looked around at her friends, every one of them looking at her with love in their eyes. To think she'd tried to keep her pregnancy from them. She was so glad they were a part of it now. She smiled through her tears. "Look what you did, turning me into a blubbering mess! At least I won't be a blubbering bride. I think I'll be out of tears by then."

"Yeah, right!" Claire exclaimed.

"I will, I swear," Hailey said. She sat down and blew her nose. Claire ran to get a small wastebasket, offering it to her. She tossed her tissue in. "Going back in for the next beautiful note."

Hailey read on, wiping away tears to take in Lauren's sweet note. She'd married Josh's younger brother Alex. The next note was from Carrie, a sweet nurse who had gone way past what Hailey would've suggested in finding a man. And then Ally, her partner in Love Junkies, who apparently knew Hailey was pregnant this whole time since they shared an office. Guess her frequent bathroom breaks and constant nibbling of saltine crackers had given her away.

She looked up at Ally with a smile. "Good job keeping my secret."

Ally hugged her. "Congratulations, baby mama! We all knew you and Josh were meant to be, even though you gave each other hell getting there."

The women murmured in agreement.

Hailey laughed. "Josh was just playing with me. Little did I know at the time. You remember how mad I'd get at him?"

"Tiny banana rings a bell," Carrie said with a grin.

Everyone laughed. That had been a good move, hinting Josh had a tiny banana. He had been beside himself trying to deny it without being obscene. Ha-ha-ha. Luckily, it wasn't true at all.

Hailey bit back a smile and kept reading. Missy was next. She was probably the most guarded of her friends after a difficult childhood and an abusive ex. Now that she was married to Ben, a total sweetheart, she'd become more expressive. Oh, wow, Missy wanted to form a mom club too!

"Yes!" Hailey exclaimed, opening her arms to Missy. "I would love a mom club. I was already thinking that."

Missy laughed and hugged her. "Love you."

"Love you too." Hailey looked to all of their friends. "Of course, you're all welcome to mom events. You don't have to be a mom just mom friendly."

"We're definitely that," Ally said. "You know we all want kids. It's just a matter of time."

Hailey nodded and turned the page. This one was from Sabrina, the relationship counselor. She'd married Josh's youngest brother, Logan. Hailey braced herself. Sabrina was really good at emotional stuff and was sure to make her cry.

Hailey,
You nut! You're the one who insisted I do the whole fake-

fiancé thing and look what happened! Now I'm married to my best friend, Logan Campbell, the best husband in the entire world, and it's all your fault! Seriously, though, I love you for being the eternal optimist and staunch supporter of love. I'm thrilled you and Josh finally opened up to each other to find the love that was waiting there all along. I hoped so much you would. We all did. I'm thrilled we'll be sisters for life.

Love,
Sabrina

Hailey looked up, a lump in her throat, and Sabrina was already there, smiling at her. She hugged her tight.

"Last one, best one," Lexi quipped. "Think you can hold off on the tears long enough to read mine?" Lexi was the most jaded against men of all of them. Boy, had she fallen hard for Marcus.

Hailey smiled and turned to Lexi's sweet note, finally closing the journal with a satisfied sigh. She stood, placed the precious journal on the chair, and opened her arms without a word. She was quickly swallowed up by a group hug with her friends for life. She blinked to clear her vision from the tears and looked around at the faces of the women she loved. Not a dry eye in the place. Their journey together would continue through the next stage of marriage and motherhood. And, of course, they'd always have their love of romance binding them together.

Hailey smiled through her tears. "I was really freaking out before—"

"No, really?" Mad said with a smile.

Hailey laughed. "I was so caught up in the details. The flowers, the gown, the food, blah, blah, blah. You ladies reminded me the most important thing is love." Her voice choked. "And I have an abundance of that from all of you and from Josh. I can't wait to marry him."

"We know!" the women chorused.

Everyone laughed.

"Let's get this pregnant bride ready," Mad said.

"Yes," Hailey said, proud to own her pregnancy. She was thrilled about it and so was Josh. Soon they'd be married, and she couldn't wait to see what Josh had planned for the honeymoon. It was the one thing she'd asked him to do.

8

Josh waited by the altar with his best man, Jake, and his groomsmen, his brothers, and let out a breath he felt like he'd been holding all day. It was finally here. And this wedding was not cursed because there was no such thing. There was only him getting mission wedding done. Bam. Jake had confirmed the furries were out of the ballroom and the preparations for his and Hailey's reception were moving forward efficiently. The rings were securely zipped into a pocket of Max's blue velvet cape. And the word from Mad was that Hailey was doing great.

The chapel was magnificent with its soaring ceiling and an abundance of gold trim and hand-painted stucco. A truly awe-inspiring space for their wedding. The chapel had once been closed to commoners and now they'd be married there. Unbelievable! The sides of the chapel held multiple apostle figures and various royal markings. Hand-carved pews, a long aisle for his beautiful bride, and three elaborate gold-trimmed organs with long silver pipes too. Fit for a princess like Hailey and, by God, he would be her prince as best he could.

He smiled to himself in anticipation of Hailey's surprise over the flowers. Mission flowers accomplished too. Gone were the leftover, wilting flower arrangements the florist had tried to pass off on them. Early this morning, he'd had Mad find some willing volunteers to scour the island for wildflowers and anything that looked beautiful and in bloom. The resulting vibrant bouquets worked in a cheerful contrast to all the white and gold trim of the chapel.

While Mad was busy rounding up the flowers, Josh had recruited a crew to join him in the kitchen to prepare the reception food. They had all the ingredients; they'd just needed extra hands. Of course, he'd only done that for their wedding. The furries could fend for themselves.

The majestic pipe organ began the processional march. Hailey's bridesmaids were his brothers' wives. It was easier to match them all that way to keep the bridal party even. One by one, his sisters-in-law walked slowly down the aisle, but his eyes kept to the very end of the aisle, waiting for the moment when Hailey finally emerged.

He straightened, the blood rushing through his veins in anticipation as Mad took her trip down the aisle, holding Max and Rose on a leash. That meant Hailey was next. The dogs wore matching blue velvet capes and appeared to be smiling, if dogs could smile. Rose had a white sprig attached on top of her cape, more of a symbolic flower girl. She'd probably eat flower petals given the chance.

Mad reached the end of the aisle, passed off Rose to Sabrina, scooped up Max, and took the rings from his cape. She handed them to Jake and stood in place on the bridal side with Max at her feet. Max barked to go see Rose, and Mad let go of his leash. Max ran straight to Rose, where Sabrina quickly scooped him up.

The music changed to the traditional wedding march, and he finally saw her. His eyes unexpectedly stung, overwhelmed with the love he had for her, his heart thumping hard. She'd chosen to walk down the aisle alone. Her dad had passed long ago and she didn't want or need a substitute. She'd always been very independent, his warrior princess.

He swallowed over the lump in his throat. Her veil didn't cover her face. Her pale blue eyes fixed on his, smiling just for him, glowing with happiness. *Yes.* This was what he'd wanted for her. Her veil hung in a long trail down her back. The gown was white satin, sleeveless, snug to her body above the waist and then tapering to a soft bell shape. A long train trailed behind her. His beautiful bride.

She reached him, finally, and he couldn't help but touch her, cupping her cheek. "Hailey, love."

She leaned into his hand. "Josh, my forever love."

His chest ached. He'd never known he could love like this, so deeply he felt it in his bones. He loved her more every single day.

The minister began the ceremony, the words tumbling around them. Josh's focus was solely on her. He moved as if in a dream, vowing to love her for all time, the words a formality to him. He'd committed heart and soul the moment she'd agreed to spend her life with him. He slid the plain gold band on her finger and gazed into her eyes. She was crying, but they were happy tears.

Finally it was official. Husband and wife.

She threw her arms around his neck with a happy cry, and he kissed her with all the love he felt, tenderly, reverently, like no one and nothing else mattered more to him than her.

Their friends and family applauded.

Hailey beamed at him. "We did it! I love you, husband."

He hugged her and spoke near her ear, his voice rough with emotion. "I love you, wife."

She pulled back to look at him. "Party time. Ready?"

He nodded, took her hand, and they walked back down the aisle together. He couldn't help his wide smile as he took in all the smiling cheering faces of the friends and family they loved. Time for the next step in their journey. United by love, nothing would stand in their way.

He'd make sure of it.

~

Hailey arrived with Josh in the gorgeous ballroom and merely gaped. The room itself with its glossy inlaid wooden floors, crystal and gold chandeliers, frescoed ceiling paintings, and gold leaf wallpaper was already stunning, but the thing that made her gape were the long buffet tables full of food.

She turned to Josh. "I thought the caterers went on strike and the chef refused to cook." She lowered her voice. "I really thought we'd just have some cold appetizers."

Josh smiled proudly, his chest puffing out. "I organized a crew to work the kitchen this morning. Sabrina was a big help. She knows cooking. We had the food; we just needed extra hands."

"So that's where you were this morning!" She hugged him and pulled back, smiling and admiring the food again. "Thank you! Let me know who did what, so I can thank them personally."

"Sure. Mad did the flower crew."

"Really? I thought maybe Bonnie's florist came through at the last minute."

Josh snorted. "Not likely. These flowers were all local and handpicked."

Realization dawned. "That's why no one had time to spend with me today! Everyone was working behind the scenes to make this wedding great. Oh, Josh! It means so much more this way, knowing our closest friends and family were involved." Her voice choked. "It's like the wedding is filled with everyone's love."

"Absolutely."

She hugged him again, still in shock at the way everything had come together in the end so beautifully. She pulled away. "It sure is quiet. What happened to the musicians?"

He looked around. "I don't know. I'll find out."

"No. Don't worry about it. Let's just mingle with everyone. I have so many people to thank!"

They made the rounds, stopping to talk, hug, and thank every single person there. Hailey even hugged and thanked the reporters. Honestly she was so happy, so filled with love, it just poured through her. She couldn't remember ever feeling so loving in her entire life. And it was all because she had the love of the most wonderful, selfless, generous man in the world.

She'd just sat down to a delicious lobster salad appetizer when the musicians filed in. Her eyes widened. They looked like Vikings from medieval times, wearing protective armor over their shoulders and chest and leather gauntlets on their forearms. Under the armor, they wore gold tunics and light brown loose trousers that ended below the knee, long wool socks, and leather boots. At least they carried instruments and not shields.

Josh shot out of his seat, and she grabbed his arm, shaking her head. He sat again and turned to her. "Hailey."

"No. We're going to enjoy the music. Of course the musicians were delayed due to a Viking reenactment on our wedding day."

He speared a shrimp on his plate. "Guarantee you this was another of Bonnie's blunders."

Phillip strode over to the musicians, speaking to them urgently.

"See?" Hailey said serenely. "Phillip is handling it."

Phillip gestured for Bonnie to join them, and they had an intense conversation. A few minutes later, a pile of armor appeared to the right of the musicians' area, quickly taken away by some servants.

Hailey turned to Josh. "It's nice when you can just enjoy yourself because you know you already have everything you could ever want. I love you. I love that we're married. And I love that I'm carrying your child."

Josh smashed his lips together, his eyes watering.

She dropped her fork with a clatter. "I made you cry? I've never seen you cry."

He jerked his chin. "Not crying."

She hugged him. He totally was, his eyes watery and red. Her sweet loving husband.

The food was divine, the company outstanding, and the music sounded great too. She danced, she laughed, and she cried a little too at the best man and matron of honor speeches.

The photographers hovered near the head table as it was announced the cutting of the wedding cake was next. Bonnie wheeled the wedding cake over in front of the head table. It had a large silver dome over it. How royal!

Hailey kissed Josh's clean-shaven cheek. "Come on. Time for me to smash wedding cake in your face."

One corner of his mouth lifted. "I already know I'm not allowed to get cake on your dress. I'll have to get my payback later."

She laughed and led him to where the cake was arranged on a wheeled table with a white tablecloth. Bonnie handed her the cake knife with a smile.

"Thanks," she said brightly, turned, and froze as Bonnie lifted the dome off the cake with a flourish.

The cake was not the round multilayered confection she'd specially ordered. It was a long rectangular sheet cake and it read Happy Birthday Hailey.

"Are you fucking kidding me?" Josh roared.

The room hushed in shocked silence. Bonnie took a step back, her way instantly blocked by the prince. Only this time it wasn't Phillip, it was the seriously pissed off Crown Prince Gabriel.

Gabriel glared at the cake and then turned to Bonnie. "You're fired. Pack your things. I want you out on the next ferry tomorrow morning." And then he raised his voice so everyone could hear his pronouncement. "You are banned from Villroy forever."

"You can't ban me!" Bonnie screeched. "I have royal blood! My great-grandmother was a maid here and the king got her pregnant! She was sent away to have the royal bastard and we've been living in poverty ever since. We will not be cast off! I'm here to claim my rightful place!"

"You have no claim," Gabriel said coolly. He gestured to the guards, and they quickly escorted Bonnie out.

Bonnie kept hollering. "I hope this place suffers like my family suffered!"

Holy crap. Hailey wasn't cursed. This wedding wasn't cursed. The wedding planner was insane. Bonnie had deliberately sabotaged the entire thing.

The photographers captured it all. So did the reporters.

She turned to Josh and whispered, "That was a much juicier story than the pregnant bride."

He laughed and pulled her into his arms. "I knew that woman was nuts. How anyone could screw up as much as she did…it was absurd." He pulled back and smiled at her. "Should we cut the cake?"

"Yes." She cut out a long rectangle in the middle, taking the Birth from Birthday. "I figure I should eat this since I'm pregnant." She tilted her head toward the cake. "Look, now it says Happy Day Hailey."

Josh looked and that was how she smashed the cake in his face, catching him by surprise. He took it well, eating some, wiping the rest, and grinning. "Watch your pretty behind, sweetheart."

She kissed him and laughed, licking the icing from her lips. "That's your job."

EPILOGUE

Hailey woke the next morning, a married woman, feeling satisfied. She threw an arm and a leg over Josh. "You awake yet?" They'd been at the reception late, and then Josh had gone all out to make their wedding night special with glowing candles and rose petals. He'd even arranged for Rose and Max to stay with Jake and Claire so they could have uninterrupted couple time. The dogs would fly home with Jake and Claire, where they'd stay while she and Josh enjoyed their honeymoon. Prince Phillip had paid for their airfare and hotel to Paris before the wedding as a gift, so this honeymoon would be Josh's special touch. She couldn't wait to find out what he'd planned.

She ran her fingers through his rumpled hair. "Josh?"

He jerked awake, his hand clamping around her wrist, his eyes flying open. "What?"

"Time to wake up."

He released her wrist and slowly smiled, relaxing again. "You horny?"

She trailed her fingers over his bare chest. They were both still naked from last night. "Yes. But I'm also excited about the honeymoon. Where are we going? The suspense is killing me."

He cupped the back of her neck and kissed her. "It's this exotic place called Clover Park, Connecticut." That was home.

She shook her head. "Try again."

"Damn, I can't even rile you up anymore."

"I'm pregnant married Zen. What can I say? I have everything I ever dreamed of." She kissed him and beamed. "The happiest of endings."

"I guess we should just skip the trip to Italy, then."

"Aaah!"

He waved a hand lazily. "Florence, Venice, Rome, who needs them?"

She climbed on top of him. "Josh!"

He wrapped his arms around her. "Surprise."

She'd been a little worried if he'd come through on the planning stuff since that was normally her territory. She should've known he'd do it up right. He never let her down. Her steady stable husband. Her rock who rocked her world.

She peppered kisses all over his gorgeous face and felt his smile.

He rolled her under him and gazed into her eyes. "I love you, pregnant wife, my warrior princess."

"I love you, pregnant husband, my warrior beast."

He laughed low in his throat and nuzzled into her neck. She sighed, running her hands over the hard planes of his back. The heat and weight of him was glorious.

He settled between her legs, taking her in a slow thrust, his movements unhurried. His gaze was dark, intense, fierce on hers. She was lost in the raw desire in his eyes. She wrapped her arms and legs around him, their gazes locked, their breaths mingling. He accelerated the pace, and she rose to meet him, the intensity building, igniting between them. There was only heat and fire and so much love.

The buildup was so slow her release slammed into her unexpectedly, bringing him with her. He stayed buried deep inside her, his lips trailing reverent kisses along her throat and jaw before settling on her mouth.

"You're mine," he growled.

He was so good with the romantic words. She was fluent in Josh speak now. "I own you," she informed him.

He smiled widely, his face lighting up. "Hailey."

She hugged him tight and sighed the happiest of sighs.

Josh headed out with Hailey and a royal escort toward the palace entrance later that morning. Phillip was all apologies for the way things had gone down with the wedding blunders. Hailey, classy as ever, was gracious and reassuring. "Phillip, I thoroughly enjoyed myself. We both did. Please don't worry. My only concern is how this is going to affect your future business."

Just then Crown Prince Gabriel, wearing his tux as if he'd never went to bed last night, and the guards stalked through, marching Bonnie out. She was subdued; her shoulders drooped. Gabriel was stiff and still looked furious. The guards escorted Bonnie outside, probably all the way to the ferry too.

The moment the palace doors closed behind her, Gabriel announced to them, Phillip, and the assorted footmen handling their luggage, "The palace is now closed to outsiders for good!"

"Gabriel, it was only one—" Phillip started.

Gabriel whirled on his brother and slashed a hand through the air. "No more weddings. No outsiders period."

The doors creaked open, and they all turned to see who it was. Josh thought Bonnie might've come back for some last minute dig, but it was a woman with a mass of brown curls and huge white-framed sunglasses, wearing a tight sleeveless dress with giant pineapples on it.

She left her wheeled suitcase by the door and hurried over to Gabriel in her leopard-print heels. "I love this already!" Her voice was clearly American. She stood next to the dour-faced, tight-jawed Gabriel and whipped out her cell phone, snapping a selfie with him.

"The palace is closed!" Gabriel barked. "And hasn't

anyone ever told you it's rude to take one's photo without permission?"

The woman startled and then muttered, "You're the rude one yelling at a guest. Geez, I flew ten hours from Tampa for this?"

A muscle ticked in Gabriel's jaw. "Do not speak to me of feminine products. Now get out."

Josh stifled a laugh. Hailey giggled.

"Feminine?" the woman asked. "Oh! Ha-ha, not tampon, *Tam-pa*." She enunciated the word slowly and clearly. "That's where I just flew in from. It's a beautiful place." Her brows furrowed. "I'm not sure anyone would dare call tampons beautiful."

They all stared at her. *Awkward*.

The woman cupped her mouth and spoke in a stage whisper to Hailey. "He's a cranky butler."

Gabriel stiffened even more, if that was possible. "Who are you?"

The woman tossed her dark curls over one shoulder and thrust her hand out. "I'm Polly Lyon and that's no lie."

Gabriel stared at her hand and made no move to take it.

Polly finally dropped her hand. "You might be the hottest butler I've ever seen, but...that stick up your ass really kills it for me."

Everyone's heads swiveled back to Gabriel to see how he would take the pseudo-compliment.

And then Crown Prince Gabriel Rourke, that grim dour son of a bitch, cracked a smile.

Three months later, Hailey carefully edited the quotes from *Luxury Weddings* and *Bride Special* to craft the perfect marketing lines for Villroy Island if they ever got back into the destination-wedding business. It turned out Bonnie had lied and there were no other weddings planned. Her sole purpose had been to sabotage the inaugural wedding to ruin Villroy's chances as a wedding venue. How she thought that would restore her family's royal blood ties was beyond comprehension. The woman was certifiable.

Hailey would use these lovely quotes for Love Junkies too, which was still going strong. They'd picked up momentum thanks to her and Ally's efforts, along with Mad's stellar marketing plan. Hailey admired the quotes, smiling to herself. Personal experience with a deeply loving wedding could only work in her favor as a wedding planner. *Luxury Weddings*: "One look at this crazy-in-love couple could've made any wedding a success." *Bride Special*: "A classy serene ceremony and reception that radiated love."

She was much too Zen about her growing baby to dwell on the hiccups. Josh had battled manly tears when they saw the ultrasound and got the news that the baby was a girl. Her warrior beast would make a fantastic dad.

La-la-la. Please ignore the following bit of paper recycling! (If only she could shred the internet.)

Luxury Weddings

Destination Wedding or Cursed Wedding?

I'm not going to pretty it up—the debut wedding on Villroy Island was anything but glamorous. But it was full of love. And I do love romantic touches. How about a groom who works behind the scenes to pull off the reception after the caterer goes on strike? The bride who doubles as her own wedding planner right up until the vows to make up for an incompetent wedding planner, who was later banned from the island! We won't mention the furry wedding that unexpectedly took place three hours prior to the debut wedding. (See sidebar.)

Our intrepid couple pulled it off and then some, showing love was more important than any traditional detail. Did I mention the musicians were in full Viking gear, fresh from a reenactment? Or that the gown was a replacement for one that was ruined by a freak fire? How about the "Happy Birthday Hailey" cake instead of a wedding cake?

And the bride was thrown overboard at her own bachelorette party! As if that wasn't bad enough, the flowers were plucked from the side of the road when the florist couldn't deliver on the promised order. Some might've said the wedding was cursed. Not this happy invited guest. Because one look at this crazy-in-love couple could've made any wedding a success.

REDACTED BY ORDER OF HIS MAJESTY KING GABRIEL ROURKE OF VILLROY ISLAND.

I say let's give Villroy Island as a destination wedding the benefit of the doubt, provided they hire a new wedding planner. Can't beat the location!

Find out more about Gabriel Rourke in the romantic comedy *Royal Catch*! *The Bachelor* meets *Survivor* royal style!

Gabriel

I am the crown prince of Villroy, heir to a kingdom, bound by duty to marry and produce an heir.

I expected a quiet arrangement through royal channels; instead I got a palace full of women vying for my hand. And how do they "win" this barbaric game set up by my crafty mother? By figuring out how to save the kingdom's faltering economy through a series of challenges. This undignified circus is beneath a man of my stature! Proof being that a saucy, ill-mannered woman wearing body-hugging clothes is in the lead. I could never love someone like that, let alone marry her.

Anna

The plan sounded simple.

I pose as my friend, pick up her inheritance, and return with the cash to keep her out of jail. (Apparently, being a princess in hiding is no excuse for identity theft.) So, yeah, I'm not exactly royal. I'm an orphan, a self-made woman, and proud of it. Suddenly I'm in a battle royale with a bunch of crazy competitive women for "riches beyond our dreams." I'm in a time crunch, which means I need to win this competition fast. Only, that means winning over the judge, the smoldering hot grim-faced Gabriel. And now I find myself wanting to compete for more than just the money. But could a royal prince ever fall for a commoner like me?

Sign up for my newsletter and never miss a new release! kyliegilmore.com/newsletter

ALSO BY KYLIE GILMORE

Unleashed Romance <<steamy romcoms with dogs!

Fetching (Book 1)
Dashing (Book 2)
Sporting (Book 3)
Toying (Book 4)
Blazing (Book 5)
Chasing (Book 6)
Daring (Book 7)
Leading (Book 8)
Racing (Book 9)
Loving (Book 10)

The Clover Park Series <<brothers who put family first!

The Opposite of Wild (Book 1)
Daisy Does It All (Book 2)
Bad Taste in Men (Book 3)
Kissing Santa (Book 4)
Restless Harmony (Book 5)
Not My Romeo (Book 6)
Rev Me Up (Book 7)
An Ambitious Engagement (Book 8)
Clutch Player (Book 9)
A Tempting Friendship (Book 10)
Clover Park Bride: Nico and Lily's Wedding
A Valentine's Day Gift (Book 11)
Maggie Meets Her Match (Book 12)

The Clover Park STUDS series <<hawt geeks who unleash into studs!

Almost Over It (Book 1)

Almost Married (Book 2)

Almost Fate (Book 3)

Almost in Love (Book 4)

Almost Romance (Book 5)

Almost Hitched (Book 6)

Happy Endings Book Club Series <<the Campbell family and a romance book club collide!

Hidden Hollywood (Book 1)

Inviting Trouble (Book 2)

So Revealing (Book 3)

Formal Arrangement (Book 4)

Bad Boy Done Wrong (Book 5)

Mess With Me (Book 6)

Resisting Fate (Book 7)

Chance of Romance (Book 8)

Wicked Flirt (Book 9)

An Inconvenient Plan (Book 10)

A Happy Endings Wedding (Book 11)

The Rourkes Series <<swoonworthy princes and kickass princesses!

Royal Catch (Book 1)

Royal Hottie (Book 2)

Royal Darling (Book 3)

Royal Charmer (Book 4)

Royal Player (Book 5)

Royal Shark (Book 6)

Rogue Prince (Book 7)

Rogue Gentleman (Book 8)

Rogue Rascal (Book 9)

Rogue Angel (Book 10)

Rogue Devil (Book 11)

Rogue Beast (Book 12)

Check out my website for the most up-to-date list of my books: kyliegilmore.com/books

ABOUT THE AUTHOR

Kylie Gilmore is the *USA Today* bestselling author of the Unleashed Romance series, the Rourkes series, the Happy Endings Book Club series, the Clover Park series, and the Clover Park STUDS series. She writes humorous romance that makes you laugh, cry, and reach for a cold glass of water.

Kylie lives in New York with her family, two cats, and a nutso dog. When she's not writing, reading hot romance, or dutifully taking notes at writing conferences, you can find her flexing her muscles all the way to the high cabinet for her secret chocolate stash.

Sign up for Kylie's Newsletter and get a FREE book! kyliegilmore.com/newsletter

For text alerts on Kylie's new releases, text KYLIE to the number (888) 707-3025. (US only)

For more fun stuff check out Kylie's website https://www.kyliegilmore.com.

Thanks for reading *A Happy Endings Wedding*. I hope you enjoyed it. Would you like to know about new releases? You can sign up for my new release email list at kyliegilmore.com/newsletter. I promise not to clog your inbox! Only new release info, sales, and some fun giveaways.

I love to hear from readers! You can find me at:
    kyliegilmore.com
    Instagram.com/kyliegilmore
    Facebook.com/KylieGilmoreToo
    Twitter @KylieGilmoreToo

If you liked Josh and Hailey's wedding story, please leave a review on your favorite retailer's website or Goodreads. Thank you.

www.ingramcontent.com/pod-product-compliance
Lightning Source LLC
LaVergne TN
LVHW011849060526
838200LV00054B/4248